THE ENFORCER

THE FAMILY

KATRINA JACKSON

SEA PORT PRESS

Physical fights
Gory descriptions of fighting
Murder on the page
Ableist language

OF ALL THE mornings to be running on two hours of sleep

It doesn't matter that I didn't know today would be important or that I thought yesterday would be just a regular degular Tuesday; what matters is that the world is clearly conspiring against me and my blood pressure. I sent my younger sister a few threatening voicemails and text messages — none of which she's responded to, by the way. I had dinner with my boyfriends. And then I had plans to get railed all night to take my mind off the stress of my sister's extended honeymoon disappearing act. But instead of that delightful evening spent in bed, my boyfriends served me dessert with a side of "you must be fucking kidding me." Unfortunately, they were not.

"We want to have a baby with you. We want to be a family."

That was not in the plans!

All the screaming and arguing we put each other through for the rest of the night hasn't erased the shock and betrayal I feel from those sentences. I don't want a baby. I don't want kids. I want to work my ass off and then fuck until I pass out in a warm bed with at least one person who loves me unconditionally. I was very clear in my dating profile. No kids. No dogs. No moving in.

"Motherfuckers," I mumble under my breath.

"What'd I do?" Shae whines.

I look up to find my younger cousin looking genuinely hurt and tired. "You still sleeping on the couch?" I bark. She jumps at my tone. "Sorry. I'm pissed."

"Clearly. About what?"

"Stop avoiding my question."

She rolls her eyes. "It's just until I can save up enough money for a deposit for another place."

"If that's what you're waiting for, then you might as well move back into your room and just marry Steve's boring ass."

I can see her throat working overtime, swallowing whatever tart response I deserve for my early morning attitude. But then her back straightens, her hackles rise, and she begins to prepare to defend her ex. Thankfully, she realizes that being Steve's shield is beneath her; it only took a few too many years.

"Good girl," I tell her.

"Shut up," she hisses, and I smile.

"You can move in with me. I have an actual spare bedroom, and I'm never there."

Shae shakes her head. "Um, I can't afford half your rent on my wages. Not even with tips."

"Sure can't, so it's a good thing I'm not asking you for money. But if you want to leave that wet mop — and I really hope you do — then I'm going to help you."

"Oh my God," she whispers. Shae clutches the strap of her backpack and bites back a smile. Knowing her, she wants to jump on me and hug me and is *just barely* suppressing the impulse. I don't like physical intimacy I didn't initiate. I especially don't like unnecessary hugs, and this would be unnecessary. Offering Shae my spare bedroom is the easiest thing I've said in the last ten hours.

"Don't get all emo on me. You're family, and you need help. Also, I never liked Steve's ass anyway. This is a no-brainer."

Shae clutches my arm and starts jumping up and down.

"Jesus," I groan. "Can you not?"

"No, I can't not. You're amazing."

"That's true, yes."

"Thank you."

I place the hand she's not trying to strangle on her shoulder to get her to be still, and we look each other in the eye. "Is that it?" I ask, noting the dark circles under her eyes. Her skin is tinged yellow. She looks pale and sickly. "You just need a new place to stay, right? There's nothing else going on?"

Shae, Zahra, and I have always been three peas in a pod. We're the only girls in our generation of the family, surrounded by male cousins who are all older, louder, and annoying. Our mothers dressed the three of us alike, practically treating us like mismatched triplets. And since I'm a few years older than Zahra and Shae, I always thought it was my responsibility to take care of them, and I've taken my role in their lives very seriously. Too seriously, Zahra says.

That's how I know Shae is lying before she even opens her mouth.

"Yep," she says in a strained tone. "I'm fine. Once I move, I'll be perfectly fine."

I squint at her and frown. She bites her bottom lip. We both know that I can press her and make her tell me whatever she's trying to hide, and I'm seriously considering it, but I don't get the chance.

Our cell phones beep at the same time. I pull mine from my purse and frown at the screen.

"Tick. Tock."

That's all the text message says.

Shae gasps, and I roll my eyes.

"Come on, let's get this shit over with. Weirdos."

I turn toward the front of the building, and Shae's hand moves to mine. I look at her over my shoulder, and she looks much more nervous now than a few seconds ago.

I squeeze her hand and pull her forward. "We haven't done anything wrong. We'll be fine!"

I'm a much better liar than Shae.

―――

"Would you like some tea?"

I want to say no, but that's not how this is done. When Aunt Mildred offers you tea, you take it.

"Thank you," Shae and I say at the same time in the same respectful tone we learned as children.

Aunt Eunice pours the light brown liquid into the cups

on the small table in front of us. We wait until she's set the teapot on the small table to our left and then resumed her seat across the living room with the rest of the elder women in our family, including our moms, aunts, grandmother, and even our Great Great Aunt Elmina, our favorite aunt. She's lied about her age so effectively that only her and God know her date of birth, and she plans to keep it that way. According to my mom, Elmina once pulled a pistol from her purse and said she'd shoot Jesus himself if he tried to put her business in the streets.

I'm pretty sure she's one hundred and eight years old, though.

Zahra nicknamed these women the Council of Aunties. It's a funny nickname right up until you're sitting in front of them with some root tea that tastes like dirt and Dawn soap trying to figure out just how much trouble you're in.

Shae's already shaking. The tea is sloshing violently in her cup, spilling over the edges into the saucer. She always folds too easily under the weight of the Aunties' gazes, bless her heart.

I'm made of tougher stuff. I lift my cup in one hand — palm clasped around it instead of fingers laced delicately through the handle. Auntie Caroline gasps in demure shock. I tip my head back to throw the tea down my throat. I burn the shit out of my tongue, and I can feel my face heating, but I'll be damned if I sip this nasty shit. Besides, my spectacle pulls everyone's attention from Shae. I might be the only one who noticed that she just touched her lips to the rim of her cup but didn't sip, and I'm certainly not going to share that information with the family police department.

"I imagine that you two are wondering why we've called

you here," Aunt Mildred says in that haughty tone I hate but mimic in every customer service situation because it's terrifyingly effective.

"I'm gonna go out on a limb and guess this is because of Zahra."

"Watch your tone," my mother warns.

"Ma'am," I add in a more subdued voice.

Mildred smirks. "This is about your sister. Have you been able to contact her?"

I frown and deflate, but only on the inside. I can't ever let the Aunties catch me slipping. "No, ma'am."

Shae shakes her head quickly. "Last I heard, she was in N-Naples."

Not to be all *Law & Order* detective or whatever, but I file Shae's verbal stumble away for further consideration later.

"And do we know why she went there instead of returning home?" Shae's mom Karin asks.

Shae turns to her mother. "No, ma'am."

I meet my mother's eyes. I can see she's worried. "I'm sure she's fine, mama."

Elmina cackles loudly, and the entire room turns toward her. She's sitting in the center of the aunties, her rheumatic eyes aimed toward the ceiling even though she's been blind maybe as long as I've been alive. Maybe longer.

"The girl is fine. If she has any damn sense, she went to Naples to find a new man to help her get over the other one. Isn't that what y'all say?"

"We sure do," I offer with a bright smile. Mina is, by far, my favorite member of the Council of Aunties. She might even be my favorite family member, period.

"Mmmhmm. You know, when I was her age, I followed a man to Ceylon."

"Where the hell is that?" another auntie whispers.

"That man had the biggest, most beautiful, long—"

"No!" Mildred yells loud enough to make everyone but Mina jump in their seats.

I turn to catch Shae's eyes, and we smile at one another as we have so many times in situations like this. Seeing her smile, though, only makes me certain that there's *definitely* something else going on with her, no matter what she says.

Mildred clears her throat, and we turn back to her. She looks frazzled in the way only Elmina can make her. "We're worried about your sister," she says in a strained voice.

"Not me," Mina says loud enough to be heard.

I bite back a peal of laughter, and Shae tries to cover hers with a cough.

Mildred's right eye twitches. "We want you to go get her."

I start to roll my eyes, and my mother sucks her teeth. "Obviously," I say. "We'll go get her eventually, but are we really at that point already? It's only been a couple of weeks since she left Milan."

"Hardly enough time to get into any *real* trouble," Mina agrees.

"She's not responding to my phone calls, so she's out of chances with me," mom says.

I shrug. My dad says I'm needlessly combative, which is probably true, but since we're on the same page, and I got so little sleep last night — but *not* because of sex — I decide to concede this fight. "Okay. I'll start looking for flights and call my editor. I can probably get there sometime late next week."

"We've booked you two on a flight tonight."

Shae gasps.

"Tonight? We have jobs, ma'am." I add that last word hastily, my eyes darting to my mother in the corner of my vision.

"Then I guess you'll be motivated to locate her and return here as quickly as possible," Eunice says, all high and mighty.

She's the youngest auntie on the Council and loves a power trip. Needless to say, she's my least favorite.

"I...I," Shae stammers. "I can't afford this. Besides, I, um...I'm about to move."

"To where?" Auntie Karin asks.

"In with me," I answer for my cousin.

Karin doesn't even look at me. "You and Steven broke up?"

Shae's eyes dart around the room. She gulps loudly. And then, she finally nods slowly.

The entire mood in the room changes.

"Well, hallelujah, amen!" Eunice says, raising a hand into the air.

"Geraldine, you owe me a hundred dollars," Mina calls out.

"Best bet I ever lost," our grandmother says.

Shae and I watch as Nana Geraldine stands from her chair and begins to dig into her bra — her makeshift wallet. She walks across the room, counting out a stack of twenty-dollar bills and then placing them into Mina's hand.

Mina closes her eyes and rubs her thumb across the

bills. If anyone knows what a real versus counterfeit bill feels like, it's Mina, although no one in the family is willing to tell us how or why. "Thank you kindly," she says to Geraldine. The rest of the room is still buzzing with energy over the apparently good news that Shae's now single. For a room full of women who believe in the sanctity of marriage, this is a shock.

I thought Zahra and I were the only ones who hated Steve.

Our grandmother moves in front of us. She squeezes my shoulder but then cups Shae's face in her hands. She smiles and then kisses her on each cheek carefully. "Never waste your time on a man who won't use his mouth or his wallet to improve your day."

"Nana," Shae gasps.

"Oh, I'm writing that shit down," I whisper.

"Watch your language," my grandmother says before returning to her seat.

"Yes, ma'am," I laugh.

"We'll have your cousins move you while you're gone," my mom says, already on her phone.

"But I'm not packed," Shae whines.

Karin waves her hand. "Your cousins will handle it."

Shae turns to me with big, wet eyes, but all I can do is shrug. When our mothers have their minds set on something, there's no stopping them. And there isn't anything I need less than to waste useless breath trying to get them to chill out. They won't.

Besides, this is the only thing they've said today that I like. Shae's wasted enough of her time letting Steve play on her tendency to be too nice. I've watched him guilt-trip her into taking care of him for years, and I wouldn't put it past him to try and do the same while she finally left his sorry ass. Taking Shae completely out of the equation really is for the best.

"So, then it's settled. You two are on a six o'clock flight to Rome tonight. You can take the train to Naples, grab Zahra, and if you're so busy," Mildred says, focusing her gaze on me, "you'll get this handled quick as you please. Are we clear?"

Shae and I take identical deep breaths. "Yes, ma'am."

"But maybe take a little time to try some Italian noodles while you're there," Mina says.

The entire room groans, but I laugh loud as hell.

SOME MEN LIKE to fuck first thing in the morning. Some men need a good espresso to jog them into consciousness.

I prefer pain.

When Salvo said he needed someone to check on a problem Giuseppe the butcher was having, I'm sure he hoped Giulio would go, but Giulio's been hiding out in his apartment as much as possible since Zahra arrived. So, Salvo got me, and in the end, that was a good thing.

I take a leisurely stroll from my apartment through the Piazza Garibaldi before the sun is even in the sky. Salvo will probably have a fit about me walking alone by myself, but sometimes he's needlessly paranoid, so what he doesn't know won't hurt him. I enjoy prowling the city first thing in the morning when the streets are still dark and the air smells like raw flour and the sea. And trash. Okay, sometimes the city smells like trash, but that doesn't stop me from enjoying those last few moments of night.

I don't skulk in the shadows. I don't need to. The high of being able to walk through these streets in full dark like I own them — because I do, through Salvo, at least — is the best high in the world. I don't need drugs or alcohol or figa; all I need is this.

Actually, most days, all I need is the crack of my fist against someone else's jaw. There's nothing that makes me feel more powerful and human as that.

I know something's wrong as soon as I turn the corner. Even this early in the morning, something doesn't feel right. I've been surrounded by the sounds of the city coming awake around me, an echo of the cacophony of this place in full swing. The clash of metal as a large delivery truck hits a pothole, a rough curse, the faint sound of a boat in the very far distance. On this early morning stroll, these are all sounds I recognize as familiar.

Giuseppe pleading is not.

Most people learn to run away from danger while young. The first time fear ripples up their spine, something elemental, something that goes as far back as the dawn of the planet, tells them to turn around and get as far away from whatever triggered that feeling as possible. If they don't know, they learn eventually.

Not me. Fear feeds something foolish and curious inside me.

But I don't run toward danger. I'm reckless, but even I have my limits. I keep walking toward the sound of Giuseppe's pathetic voice at the same leisurely pace. I do take my hands out of my pockets and crack my knuckles while I'm far enough away that no one can hear the sound but me. But when I'm close, danger prickles over my skin, so I clench my fists and roll my neck from side to side, and I feel at ease.

That's the problem with me. This is the reason Salvo probably would have preferred to send Giulio in my place. Someone else might have run for backup or at least stopped to think through the options. Giulio probably would have done some reconnaissance, at least.

Not me.

I duck into the alleyway that runs along the side of the bakery and am rewarded by two things immediately. Salvo didn't know what Giuseppe's problem was — the old man was too nervous to say — which is why he wanted to send Giulio to get to the bottom of the issue. That would have taken time. But my method of running headfirst into danger also works. I hear Giuseppe's nervous stammering, and his wife's pleas, and a thug threatening him. Even I can put two and two together: Giuseppe's being shaken down.

My second reward comes in that moment of triumph that I solved the mystery all on my own.

And now that I know what's going on, I can do what I do best.

When the old men talk about getting into fights, they focus on the pain of getting hit, but that's not the full picture. There's also the crack of skin, meat, and muscle when fists collide; when you feel someone else's skin give way under your blow, the slick splatter of blood and spit hitting the concrete when you shake off one punch in preparation for another. I don't mind getting hit, but I prefer to hit — who doesn't — and I could talk about it all day. My perfect recall never lets me forget a single fight I've been in, not one blow I've taken or given. I remember it all. I feel it all, still.

When he sees me, this skinny fuck I don't recognize

releases Giuseppe's collar and backs away because he understands fear; he knows that the best thing he can do — the only option in this tight alley — is to back away from the big hulking monster with the sick smile on his face. Me. I shrug out of my coat and drop it on the ground. Giulio likes expensive things, not me — I'd only ruin them with sauce or wine or blood.

I watch the other man as he tries to get his bearings and figure out who I am, why I'm here, and if he can take me down on his own.

He can't.

I hear Giuseppe and his wife pleading for something, but I don't listen. I hear the blood in my veins, my pulse slow and steady, the sound of my shoes on the gravel, and his panting breaths. He sounds like a cornered animal because even if his brain doesn't know it yet, he is.

When he comes for me, it's a desperate play to punch past me and run. I appreciate the nerve so much that I let his blow land. It's like getting hit by a child, and that, more than anything, annoys me.

This bambino fragile is shaking someone down in my territory? How disrespectful.

I return his punch and feel the contact travel from my knuckles and up my arm in a comforting vibration. The air leaves his mouth in a pained groan. These familiar sensations bring me fully awake and almost make up for that terrible punch.

Almost.

He crumbles to the ground, and I back away from his grip, still standing between him and his escape. I give him a moment to catch his breath, but not too long.

"Alzati," I say in a calm voice that Giulio sometimes says scares even him. But this is me being kind, giving him a warning he doesn't deserve because this is my morning routine; this fight is how I'll welcome the day.

I could write an essay on the moment I know that this asshole isn't trying to collect himself but is plotting on how to take me down. I was terrible in school, though, so maybe I couldn't write that essay, but believe that I know. It's in the way his body stills as I circle him and the slight tilt of his head as he tries to keep me in his line of sight.

And I can tell you the moment he makes a critical error. It's when he lets me circle behind him. I can imagine he just needs a few more seconds to catch his breath, but none of us is promised a few more breaths in this life, and a single inhalation is more than enough time to die.

Once I'm out of his peripheral vision, I reach for him, grabbing him by the neck. I yank him into the air quickly and slam him face-first into the concrete. His nose and forehead bounce off the ground.

Giuseppe's wife begins to pray. It's a familiar prayer. My mother still says this one for me.

I don't wait until I know if he's dead or just unconscious; I sit on his back and make certain. There's a puddle of blood spreading under his face. I sigh and pull my phone from my pocket. I don't need to wake Salvo or Giulio for this part because it's the kind of situation they would call *me* to handle.

I have a friend with a delivery truck who'll dispose of this body, and he just happens to be nearby. I don't ask why, and he doesn't offer an explanation, which is exactly the kind of friendship I value.

"Andare all'interno," I say to Giuseppe.

The old man opens his mouth as if he's about to ask something he doesn't need — or want — to know, but his wife stops him. I look at her, and she nods once in my direction before pulling her husband inside their bakery. Apparently, prayers aren't the only thing Giuseppe's wife has in common with my mother.

I only have to wait a quarter of an hour before my friend arrives, and he's gone in less time than that. I knock on the bakery's back door and ask for a bucket of water to douse the puddle of blood. In less than an hour after I arrived, Giuseppe's problem is handled.

I emerge back onto the sidewalk from the alley to find Giuseppe's wife sweeping the storefront as if this is a regular morning. She stops when she sees me, and I nod in her direction this time, keeping my distance as I do with my own mother.

She nods in return and holds up a hand, telling me to wait.

I shouldn't. The sun is brightening the sky. The faster I'm on my way, the better. But I wait, thankfully not long. She returns with a bag, and I can smell the fresh bread and hot sugar inside.

"Hai un debole per i dolci," she says.

"How'd you know?" I ask.

She shrugs, and that's the end of our conversation.

I watch her for a few seconds I can't spare, and she picks up her broom, resuming her work as if I'm no longer here. After a short while, I turn and head back home. I don't go the way I came; that wouldn't be wise. I never want to give someone more than one chance to see me.

I clutch my bag of pastries in one hand, shove the other into my pocket — to hide the red bruises on my knuckles — and walk toward Piazzi Garibaldi. I could rush home to put my clothes in the wash, I'm almost certainly covered in blood splatter, but rushing invites too much attention; rushing is how you get caught.

So, I walk leisurely to the square. I stop at a café on the way and buy a cappuccino. I use my uninjured hand to pay.

In the piazza, I find a seat, sip my coffee, eat a pastry or three, and I watch as Naples comes to life around me. It looks like the beginning of a beautiful day.

WE MAKE it to Roma Termini and thankfully manage to snag a couple of tickets on the next train to Naples. It's still early morning. In a perfect world, Shae and I will get to Naples before lunch, find Zahra before nightfall, and be back on a plane tomorrow afternoon.

I don't care how big Naples is. I don't care that there are more details missing from that plan than men leering at us on the train platform. My mother raised Zahra and I to believe that, in the absence of good sense, reckless hope was also effective.

Shae never quite took to that lesson.

When I turn to her, I'm not surprised to find Shae looking nervous and a little sweaty. It's a warm summer morning, and we've lugged our jetlagged bodies and luggage through clumps of tourists at the airport, commuter traffic at the train station, and down a flight of surprisingly steep stairs to arrive at our platform. My conviction that something is absolutely going on with my younger cousin has only intensified during this trip. As soon as we find Zahra, I'm going to figure out what she's hiding from me. But until then, all I can give her is a gentle, and maybe empty, platitude.

"Everything's going to be alright," I tell her, even though I have no idea what we're up against.

When she looks up at me, I can see that the dark circles under her eyes seem to have deepened in color and begun to take over more of her face.

"I promise."

She smiles sadly. "We're not kids anymore, Zoe. You can't fix the world for me."

"The fuck I can't," I say as our train's arrival begins to flash on the screen above us.

I pretend to work on the ride to Naples.

I thought my editor would be pissed at my sudden departure from the country and the brief email explaining why, but when we land in Rome, she's sent me a bunch of ideas for stories I might like to write about.

None of them sound interesting, and I don't plan to be in Europe long enough to do any actual research, but I spend the train ride toward the coast scrolling through other people's stories so I can pretend to have done my due diligence. I also want to take my mind off of everything at home. And because the universe is conspiring to exhaust me, I get the email notification at the worst possible moment.

"What's this about you leaving the country? Zoe, are you
  serious? Are you really going to let it end like this?"

I read Tyrone's email more times than is necessary. I
understand his question. I understand why he's mad. I don't
understand how to tell him that yeah, I'm seriously going to
let it end like this. As far as I'm concerned, they made this
decision, not me.

A year ago, I thought I'd spend a good decade or so with
Tyrone and Kevin. I had an entire plan for my life that
included them, but only as much as we all agreed. We did
not agree on kids, though, so now I have to rethink my entire
life. Alone. I'm not a crier, but I do get choked up reading
and rereading his email. I loved them. I'd been happy with
them. But I don't know what else there is to say between the
three of us.

I don't want kids. They do. Where are we supposed to
go from here?

Nowhere.

Or Italy, apparently. I text my mother to let her — and
by extension, the rest of the Council of Aunties — know
that we've made it to Italy, and we're on our way to Naples.
I hope she doesn't respond. I can't handle Tyrone's email
and communicating with my mother so close together. Not
today. As much as my mother was willing to acknowledge
my relationship, she would frown at me, suck her teeth, and
accuse me of being greedy and afraid of commitment.

For the record, I'm not. Well, not in the way that my
mom thinks. I am greedy, but it is my personal opinion that
every person should be greedy with their joy. There can
never be *too much* joy as far as I'm concerned. And I love

my mother, but I won't let her shame me for that. And while she knows me very well, of course, my mom also still sees me as an extension of her. Whenever my life veers off the path she's laid out for me, she freaks out. That's why she thinks I'm commitment-phobic when really, I am desperate to have people to spend my life with.

It's the people part that freaks my mother out. I imagine she'll be happy to know that I've broken up with Tyrone and Kevin. She probably won't care at all that I'm bereft.

I don't want to think about this anymore.

"Oh, shit," I hiss.

"What?" Shae has been drifting in and out of sleep, but she wakes with a start.

I pat her right hand. "Nothing's wrong," I reassure her. "I just remembered that I had a way to find Zahra quickly."

"You do?"

I nod and turn back to my phone. I start typing the text I would have sent yesterday if my relationship hadn't imploded and my family wasn't supremely strange.

"KeKe, any word on my sister?"

I'm hoping for a fast response, and I get it.

"Yep. Sending the report now. She hasn't spent any money recently, but a friend of a friend of an NSA agent says her phone is still in the city. And since you're on your way to Naples..."

I sigh and shake my head.

"Please stop tracking my phone."

"No can do. Have some pasta for me."

"Is everything okay?" Shae asks.

I open my laptop, "Yeah, everything's fine. I had KeKe track Zahra's credit card. I figure we can check into the hotel, go to the last place she spent money, and then..."

"And then what?"

I cringe and shrug, and we both laugh.

"This entire trip is a half-assed idea pretending to be an actual plan. We're rolling with the punches, okay?"

"Okay. Do you think she's really in danger, or are the Aunties being paranoid?"

I roll my eyes. "The Aunties are always doing the most. She's fine. We'd know if she wasn't. But apparently, whatever — or whoever — she's doing made her forget how to send a goddamn text message."

"Do you think she'll be happy to see us?"

"Absolutely fucking not," I laugh. "But all she had to do was reach out, and we could have stayed home. If she were being less Eat, Pray, Radio Silence, we could be back home moving your stuff into my apartment right now."

Shae winces. "I hate moving."

"Well, then, you can thank her when we get there. She might like that. And if you distract her, I'll hit her over the head, and we can drag her into a taxi, and there," I dust my hands together, "trip over. See how this plan is coming together?"

"Like a crime? Because it sounds like a crime to me," Shae laughs.

"A criminal plan is *still* a plan."

Shae and I laugh together again, and I feel like everything really will be okay.

———

Zahra

"Amore, torna a letto," Giulio yells from the bedroom.

"I need to hydrate. You need food. We can't live on sex alone," I laugh before I drink an entire large bottle of water. I'm joking, but I'm also not. Giulio and I have been doing nothing but having sex when he's home, and it's great. I mean, it's entirely unsustainable. I have a job and a life back home that I'm still running away from. Giulio also has a life and some kind of job here that he's also avoiding whenever he can. We're using sex as our primary means of avoidance even though we both know eventually it'll all have to come to an end.

But that's a problem for another day, some other morning, and I don't want us to be at that day yet. So, I go back to bed like he asks. And hey, if nothing else comes of all this, at least my Italian's getting a little better!

"This is beautiful," I say, staring at maybe the third gorgeous square we've stumbled through on our way from our hotel to the address KeKe sent me.

Shae nods, but she's not paying attention. If I didn't know her better, I'd think she was running scared from the cops, the way she's looking from left to right. But Shae can't even steal a candy bar without freaking out about going to jail and confessing all her sins — and incriminating Zahra and I right along with her. I wanted to throttle her as a child for being the worst accomplice ever, but as an adult, her innocence is one of the things I love most about her.

"Girl, what the hell is going on with you?"

"Huh?"

I roll my eyes. "Don't 'huh' me. What is up with you?"

"Nothing. I'm hungry. Tired?"

"Which is it?"

"Both?"

I stop walking and grab her forearm. I try and look her

in the eyes, but she won't meet my gaze, which isn't so out of the ordinary, but this entire trip has been so strange that it's hard to read her distraction in any other way besides deeply confusing, and maybe even a little bit scary.

"Okay, what the fuck is going on right now?" I explode.

Shae jumps at the sound of my voice.

"Look," I say carefully, letting her arm go. "I don't want to press you. It's not my business, but..." My eyes go to her stomach. I think about all of our girly dreams to be just like our mothers, attached at the hips and raising our children side by side. Even me, the person who didn't want children — I still wanted to be right there as my little sister and cousin inevitably had theirs. I've been preparing to be the best carefree, rich auntie to ever show up at the cookout with a bottle of champagne, a store-bought cake, and a new man on her arm since I was twelve. This has been my goal, but in my mind, I thought we'd all be older, settled, and surer of ourselves. I certainly never thought that Shae would tie herself to someone as basic as Steve. I mean, Shae deserves better. More.

And so do I.

Something about the way Shae's avoiding my eyes as if she can feel my failure cuts me deep. It's as if she knows how it hurt, how hard that shock reverberated, when Kevin asked me to get pregnant even though I'd always been very clear that kids were not just off the table, there was no table for that discussion at all. As if she'd been next to me on the train uptown with a dry, scratchy throat and watery eyes, stubbornly refusing to let even a single tear drop. So, now I'm avoiding her eyes.

We're looking everywhere but at one another as we resume our hunt for Zahra. We listen to the voice commands on the app leading us through Naples's streets, holding our secrets closer to our chests than before. I want to believe that every step brings us closer to Zahra, but that's just the quarterly dose of unfounded optimism hitting my veins because I'm too tired to drown it out with cynicism. But eventually, this kind of naïveté will fade, and what if we haven't found Zahra before it does? Then what will I do?

This train of thought is ruining my mood and feels wholly out of place considering the beautiful city around us.

"Your destination is on the left."

Instead of looking left, I look down at my phone, but Shae's gasp pulls my eyes to her.

"Oh my God."

I look at her and then across the paved square to the restaurant and back again. Shae's stopped walking, and I turn around in confusion. "What's up? Did you see her?"

I turn around in a circle, looking everywhere for Zahra and seeing her nowhere. I feel like I'm going insane. It's probably just jet lag, but I don't care. It's been a weird couple of days, and the red-faced nervous look on Shae's face is freaking me out, so I take off.

"Zoe," Shae calls after me, but I don't stop. I stomp across that brick square toward the restaurant.

I can hear Shae running after me, even as my name sounds more unhinged each time she says it. I pull the door open — a little dramatically — and rush inside a very normal restaurant. It looks like something out of a quaint movie set. It's actually a little disorienting if I'm honest. Two seconds ago, I felt like there was pure panic running through my veins, but when I step into this place, a sense of calm settles over me. But that's probably because of the quiet.

I scan the room, and it's mostly empty, full of far more chairs than people. There's a gray-haired man sitting at a small table in the corner, peering at me over the top of his newspaper. I can hear the sounds of people in the kitchen, but when I look in that direction, I find a white man with light brown hair leaning forward on the bar staring at me. Hard. The look on his face is the definition of thirsty, so I roll my eyes and look away. There's a waitress at a table to my left taking orders.

But that's it. There's no Zahra.

This is fine. It's not a sign of my failures accumulating one on top of the other. It's only the first day, we haven't even been in the country for twelve hours, but I'd let myself imagine that it could be that easy, which is so unlike me. Yeah, jet lag is really about to kick my entire ass on this trip. The only way to save myself is to find my foolish little sister quick and get back to the States before my body can fully acknowledge that I've left home.

I turn around, looking for my cousin, and I see her standing outside in the square, her eyes and mouth wide in shock — as if she's afraid to get too close to the door. I shake my head and push the door open. "Shae, what the hell? She's not here. What is going on?"

She's biting her bottom lip and wringing her hands. She looks worse than just after she threw up on the airplane. She's looking past me, though, and I feel as if she and I are living in two different universes.

It's not until the front door of the restaurant bangs open

behind me that I realize how badly I've been misreading my cousin for the past few hours.

Some investigative journalist I am.

I THOUGHT, after this morning, today might be boring. Slow, even. But Giulio says I'm easily bored, so maybe I just assumed that nothing could top the excitement of my encounter behind Giuseppe's bakery. I'm not disappointed that I'm wrong, especially not when she walks through the door, but that brief moment of interest is almost immediately smothered by panic.

I yell at Salvo not to go outside. He doesn't listen to me all the time, but he has an unusually thorough understanding of how dangerous the world is, so I never normally have to tell him not to rush out into the day to follow some unknown woman, even if she does look to be one hundred and eighty centimeters of nothing but curves. Even *I* didn't do that.

I did think about it. But that's not the point.

I scramble over the bar, which is no easy feat considering that running and jumping are more Giulio's strengths. I'm a punch and duck away kind of man, but if something happens to Salvo, I'll be a dead kind of man.

I burst through the front door, and the sun burns my eyes. I don't squint, though. I keep Salvo in my peripheral vision and scan the square. I've never missed Giulio more than at this moment. He could have pulled Salvo back inside, and maybe even the woman he followed, while I do what I do best. I can't do both, however, so I look for threats and pray that Salvo will remember himself.

I'm lucky. I see the gun before he fires. If Giulio were here, he'd have pulled his own gun from...somewhere and handled this casually, but I'm not armed. Not with a gun, anyway. So, I do what I always do and use my body as the weapon it is.

I see the gun, and I head straight for it.

Most people with guns shouldn't have them; they have no idea what they're doing, and they usually want to take the easy way out, the distance letting them pretend that the mess and the gore won't touch them. But I live for the mess and the gore and everything in between. So, when people point a gun at me, I consider it my mission to make sure they never think about doing that again.

His eyes widen when he realizes I'm rushing toward him — my body between the barrel of this gun and my boss. If he was a smart man — no, I see the closer I get, boy — he'd shoot me in the forehead. The chest, at least. But his hand is shaking. He lets me get close enough to see sweat on his brow.

Mistake for him. Exciting development for me.

He should pull the trigger. As I stalk closer, I think that thought like a chant.

Premere il grilletto.

Premere il grilletto.

Sparare.

Sparare.

Shoot.

It's the smart thing to do if he wants to live. But if I know anything, it's that the line between people who will do anything to live and those who won't is not thin, and I place myself squarely on the former side. I don't mind fighting to live.

The fighting is probably my favorite part.

I've been shot, stabbed, beaten more times than I can count. I was even run over once. That was interesting. I know it's going to take more than one bullet to slow me down, so I hope he shoots me. I would have more respect for him if he did.

Unfortunately for both of us, he does not.

Faster than he expects — because I'm so big — I'm close enough to reach for him. I don't miss. When I grab his hand, I feel every bone break in my grip, but I squeeze to make sure. He screams, but when I slam my fist into the side of his face, all I hear is the crunch of bones and nothing else for an immeasurable amount of time; it could be five seconds or five hours, I don't know, and I don't care. What I know is the moment when the hand holding his gun collapses in my palm, and his gun clatters to the ground. I know the second the bones on the left side of his face give way.

These moments are like a pure shot of adrenaline to my brain.

I let him go, and he crumples to the pavement, whimpering and holding his ruined hand. I kick the gun out of the way and then grab him by the front of his shirt, ready to keep punching him. It feels good.

"Alfonso."

Salvo calls my name in a sharp clip that cuts through the bloodlust. Unfortunately.

I turn to look at him over my shoulder with raised eyebrows, annoyed but ready for some orders now that he's hopefully pulled himself together. By the look on his face, I'm not sure that he has — not fully, anyway. But he has himself together enough to nod toward the restaurant. I don't need him to speak to get the gist of that gesture.

I grab the gun and shove it into the back of my trousers, and then I haul the man up from the ground and over my shoulder. I turn to Salvo and nod my head toward the front of the restaurant.

He turns to the woman who rushed into the restaurant earlier and a woman next to her. I've never seen either of them before, but they remind me of Zahra. I don't know if it's okay to think that, though, and there are more important things to do in this moment, in any case.

I do notice that Salvo is speaking only to one woman, but not the one I saw in the restaurant. He's inching close to her, his hands reaching, and his voice is so soft and gentle that for a second, I don't even recognize him. I look at the other woman, and we make eye contact. She looks as confused about whatever is happening right now as I am.

"Follow Alfonso, please," Salvo says. No, he pleads. And my eyebrows lift in surprise.

Salvo is different from the other bosses I've met. He's gentle, doesn't raise his voice, and makes requests even of low-life gangsters still wet behind their ears instead of barking out orders. Sure, it's all a façade because, just like the other bosses, Salvo has no problem killing an enemy. In fact, he's even better — scarier — because he doesn't have a problem taking out his enemies with his own hands, and he never needs to raise his voice above a whisper while doing so.

But even with the gentler touch, Salvo doesn't plead. He doesn't beg. An hour ago, I thought he'd never beg, not even with a gun to his head, but apparently, I was wrong.

I look at Salvo, but he only has eyes for this woman. I want to ask what the hell is going on right now, but I'm standing in the middle of the square with a half-dead man over my shoulder, and I've been standing in this exact spot for far too long. I turn toward the entrance to the alleyway that runs along the side of the restaurant casually, shifting the dead weight to one shoulder as if this isn't a strange thing to be doing whatsoever. I pull my mobile from my pants pocket and call Giulio.

"Ciao," he says, laughing through the word. His voice sounds lighter than I've ever heard before. He's happy. I hear Zahra's laughter in the background, and I feel terrible.

I have three brothers, and Giulio is as close to me as any of them. I hate to break up whatever beautiful morning they've been sharing, but in our line of work, I cannot afford to be so kind.

"You need to get to the restaurant," I say. "Now."

I hang up before he can answer. There's nothing else to say. We both know what kind of life we live. As I plunge into the darkness of this familiar alley, I turn around to find the tall, thick woman following behind me with big, scared eyes. She's staring forward but not really seeing, not until I grunt under my breath. Her gaze shifts, her eyes focus on me, and she frowns. I smile at her, and her frown deepens. For whatever reason, that pleases me.

I lift my eyes to look past her to see the other woman and Salvo behind her. Close behind her. Their eyes are shifting to one another. Whatever is going on between them cannot be good.

My DAD SAYS that I didn't inherit anything from him besides his height and a love of punk rock music, and he's right; in every other way, I am my mother's child. That means that I am preternaturally suspicious in all situations, and I hate feeling as if I don't know what's going on. So, this moment is making my anxiety spike. But unlike my mother, I had a father who taught me how to manage this kind of stress. My mom rages and throws a tantrum until she feels in control of a moment, but dad taught me to observe. If the only thing that I can control is myself — and I didn't want to be extra as fuck like mom — dad taught me how to lock myself down for as long as I need and take in the fullness of my surroundings to give my brain time to process something besides fear.

So, here's what I know:

Blood has been shed in this room. Lots of it. The sharp metallic scent of it lingers in the air, but it's just barely covered over by the sting of industrial cleaning solutions. My own blood wants to race at the smell. It's so strong that I have to breathe through my mouth to lessen the impact. The room is a rectangle, maybe seven feet by ten, with a single bare lightbulb hanging from the ceiling. There's a metal table in the center, and the big brute throws the bloody man he punched into unconsciousness atop it. I thought he was dead, but then I hear a rattled, raspy breath, followed by a pained cough and the spray of blood onto the floor.

This is a room for torture. I once wrote an exposé on Russian mobsters, and I've watched all the *Saw* movies at least twice, so I know what I'm seeing. I know what's up, but I can't get caught up thinking about any specific detail, or I'll panic like it seems Shae is. My cousin is holding herself in the corner, trembling, her eyes darting left and right, but I can't focus on that either.

There are two doors; one we've just come through that I know leads to the alleyway, and another that obviously leads into the building where the restaurant is housed. I wonder if that door is closed. Or locked. I wonder if I can grab Shae's hand and leave through the door we entered. I wonder how long we could survive before whoever the fuck sent the dude on the table came looking for us. I wonder where in the actual fuck my little sister is.

I get one answer, at least.

The door to the alleyway bursts open, and a dark-haired man with a nice smattering of day-old scruff rushes inside before pulling my little sister into the room behind him. To be honest, this is the least surprising thing that's happened in the past twenty minutes.

"Oh my God," Zahra says. "What are you doing here?"

She's looking between me and Shae with a surprised

smile that falls into a grimace. "Damn. The Council sent y'all, huh?"

Shae is too busy looking toward the door that leads into the restaurant — the door the older man who'd barely been able to tear his eyes from her had exited through a few minutes ago. He'd grabbed her waist and whispered something I couldn't pick up from across the room before he'd gone.

So, Zahra turns to me for answers.

"Of course, they sent us," I say, each word making me feel more like myself. "Now tell me what the fuck is going on."

"What do you mean?" Zahra says. "I just got here. How would I know?"

I love my little sister. I also know when she's lying through her teeth. I glare at her to remind her that, shock or not, we can still scrap. She knows what my threats look like; no words necessary.

She edges behind the man with the dark hair. "Really," she whines, "I don't know."

"Ah," he says, stepping to the side and exposing her to my gaze. She glares at him with her hands on her hips. "Is this your sister?"

"Yes," Zahra says testily. "Now, could you please stand between us? Zoe likes to fight."

"Veramente?" the big brute who beat that guy with the gun like he was a rag doll asks.

But I'm not worried about anyone else in this room besides Zahra right now. We stare at one another like we used to when we were kids, with a silent tension that will either bubble over into laughter or a full-fledged brawl.

Only God knows what's coming next, but I'm betting it isn't laughter, and the entire room is quiet as my sister and I have a stand-off.

We could have lasted at least an hour, I think, but after a couple minutes, the other man walks back into the room and draws everyone's attention to him, even mine. I can read a room. He is definitely the boss. But what trips me up and pulls Zahra to my side is that he only has eyes for Shae.

"Girl, what'd I miss?" Zahra whispers to me. I turn and glare at her, and she shrugs with wide eyes. "What? Sal's looking at her like..."

"Like what? And who the fuck is Sal?"

"Him, obviously."

"Are you dim? Did that man fuck the brains out of you? Is that why you haven't called me back?"

Someone snickers.

"I meant to call," Zahra says. "I was going to call, just not yet."

"Imagine," I say, raising my voice since everyone can hear us anyway. "Imagine if you had just sent that text message or email. Fuck, a voice note probably would have appeased the Aunties, and we wouldn't have had to come all the way here and immediately get caught in the middle of some dude trying to shoot somebody."

Zahra's dark-haired man starts speaking quickly, but it's all in Italian, so I ignore him.

"And then," I keep going, "that big motherfucker beat that dude to death."

"He's alive," the man says simply.

"Calm down," the older man says, pulling our eyes to him briefly, but no one listens to him. The dark-haired one is ranting in Italian, looking between the older man and the brute, and I go back to giving Zahra the piece of my mind that has been storing up all the annoyance my body can handle since I had to hop on a flight here under duress.

"We all realize you've been through some shit, but the least you could have done was let us know you were okay. Especially since there's a Where's Zahra blog series in the tabloids."

"There is?"

"Yes!" I scream. "Ryan came back from Italy without you, and now the papers are trying to turn you into a minor celebrity." Her face scrunches. "Yes. Exactly. And if you had just gotten back to us, the family could have handled it. That would have been the responsible thing to do."

"Why do I have to be responsible?" Zahra yells. "Maybe I just want to live my life not in a fishbowl for the first time in years. Maybe I wanted a few more weeks without you and the Aunties watching me like a hawk."

"Me? I'm just looking out for you. That's it."

"But who asked you to do that? Not me!"

"I'm pregnant." Shae doesn't raise her voice, but she might as well have. The entire room goes quiet again.

Zahra and I stop fighting and give her all of our attention, but Shae isn't looking at us at all. She's staring at the older man with wet eyes and her arms wrapped across her stomach protectively.

"How?"

Zahra elbows me. "Excuse me, what exactly have I missed?"

"Salvo," the dark-haired man says, and that's all I understand. The boss doesn't listen to him anyway. I don't know how, but he's somehow managing to look at Shae with *more* intensity.

"What is going on?" Zahra whines.

"It's not fun, is it?" I can't help but say.

She scowls at me.

"Quiet," the older man says, and the dark-haired man puts an arm around Zahra's shoulder and pulls her into his side.

I raise my eyebrows at her. "What's going on?" I mouth in silence.

"Bella," he says to Shae in a gentle rumble of a voice that gives me shivers.

Zahra and I turn to the corner, where Shae has lodged herself as if she needs something solid at her back. She looks skittish and scared, or sad. I can't tell, and I can always tell how Shae and Zahra feel normally. We watch as the gray-haired man advances on her cautiously. I can hear the timbre of his voice, but he manages to actually whisper, and whatever he says is only for Shae's ears. I watch her face for a reaction, ready to step in if she needs me.

Tears fall down her cheeks, and she nods slowly. I hold my breath as his hands move to her neck, his thumbs skim her jaw, and then he pulls her face to his.

"I really don't know what the fuck is going on here," I say.

"Me either, but this is super sweet," Zahra adds. "I mean, Steve is probably gonna be pissed about this, but—"

"She broke up with him," I say excitedly.

"Hallelujah! Amen," Zahra says, and I nod along.

"So," the big one says, "what do you want me to do with

him?" Zahra, the dark-haired one, and I turn to the unconscious man on the table.

"Not now," the dark-haired one says. "Salvo's busy."

"Oh, okay. I'll make sure the carabinieri knows not to raid us right now because he's busy seducing a pregnant American. I'm sure they'll understand."

"The carabinieri?" Zahra says.

"The cops? Alright, cute moment over. What the fuck is going on here?" I yell.

"A lot," the big one says. And that's when I hear sirens.

"ACT NORMAL," the big brute says, pulling a chair in the dining room out for me.

Whatever that means.

"Don't freak out," Zahra hisses as the dark-haired man whispers something into her ear. His mouth caresses her cheek, and she smiles in a way I *never* saw during all those years she was with Ryan.

But I cut my eyes at her. "The fuck."

Zahra rolls her eyes at me before we both turn to see the older man kneeling next to Shae's chair possessively. He only moves because the big, tall bruiser places a hand on his shoulder and says something to him in Italian. He nods and looks up at my baby cousin like she is the center of the universe.

"Goddamn," Zahra whispers.

We all watch as he stands and walks back through the restaurant with the dark-haired man. The big one appears behind the bar, picks up a clean shot glass, pours something clear into it and knocks it back. He notices me watching him, and we lock eyes. He winks at me. I roll my eyes and turn back to my family.

"I'm pregnant," Shae says again, and thank God she does. Those two words ground me in this moment and at this table with my little sister and cousin. Those two words give me a trapdoor to ignore that wink and begin to process whatever the fuck is happening around us.

"Yeah, we heard that part," Zahra says. "We'd like to know about Sal."

"Salvatore," Shae says in a tone of voice that manages to be hard but also wistful. She never said Steve's name that way.

My sister and I look at each other with raised eyebrows.

"And how do you know him?" I ask carefully, treating my cousin like one of my interview subjects.

"I've been here before."

"To Rome," I say, "with Steve."

She nods. "I came to Naples on a day trip," she says cautiously. "I-I was supposed to be with Steve, but he didn't..." She shakes her head and shrugs, almost as if she's as confused as we are — as if she can't quite remember what happened during that trip.

Zahra scoffs. "We get it. We met him. He sucked." I kick my sister under the table. She's unbothered. "The truth is the truth."

"So, you came to Naples on your own?" I ask Shae, trying to get this conversation back on track.

"And you met Sal?" Zahra asks. I sigh. She leans forward and lowers her voice. "And then you let him seduce you into having his elegant baby?"

"Are you high?" I ask her.

She shrugs at me while squeezing Shae's hand. "That man is smooth as hell. It's gotta be in his DNA. Also, yes," she says. "I've been having nothing but the best orgasms of my life for the past few weeks. I feel like a new person on an alien planet."

"See how easy that would have been to text?"

She rolls her eyes and crosses her arms like a stroppy teenager. "Here we go again."

"I didn't think," Shae says, pulling my attention to her.

"No shit," I screech. My nerves are frayed, and as usual, my little sister is tap dancing on them for the hell of it. "I gave you both the best sex education I and the internet could muster. We talked about all kinds of birth control and boundaries and how to never let a man trap you with sex or money. How did this happen?"

At this point, I'm not even really speaking to Shae or Zahra. I'm speaking to myself. Maybe I'm practicing my defense for when I have to go back in front of the Council of Aunties. I didn't do anything. I am *not* my sister's or cousin's keeper, regardless of how I behave or the responsibility they've heaped onto my shoulders. This isn't my fault.

Unfortunately, it still *feels* as if I've failed them.

A high whistle from the bar interrupts my spiral. I turn, and the big man is shaking his head at me just as the front door bursts open.

Alfonso

I love a good family drama. I grew up watching them with my aunts and grandmother, so I can appreciate a good dramatic moment. I watch Zahra and her sisters with the kind of excitement I used to feel in my nona's home. So, I hate to disrupt the moment, but I can see the police heading toward the restaurant's door, and the last thing I need is for those three to attract any more attention than they already will. Thankfully, the tall one understands my nod, and she turns to the table, reaches for a piece of bread from the basket between them, and then gestures for the other two to do the same.

"Where is he?" the cop barks at me from across the room. I've seen this one before. It's part of my job to know exactly which carabinieri work in the city and recognize them by sight, no matter their rank.

I turn to him with a blank stare, and slowly, my brows bunch into confusion. "Who?"

"You know who."

I tip my head to the side. "Are you certain?"

I know people think I'm thick, but my God, why do they make it so easy for me to toy with them?

"Where is your boss?" This question comes from Sergeant Gallo, a man who's just a little too good at his job for my liking. It's harder to frustrate him by pretending to be dumber than I am.

"I'm here," Salvo says, pushing into the room with an amiable smile on his face. "How can I be of service?"

He leans one arm on the bar and smiles warmly at the sergeant, focusing on him only. His eyes don't dart to the table across the room, and so, neither do mine. I'm not thick, but I do appreciate being able to follow his lead.

That's what I do best.

"There was a commotion in the square," Sergeant Gallo says.

"Oh?" Salvo replies in a saddened tone. He shakes his head and turns to me. "This used to be such a lovely place."

I shrug and turn back to wiping the glasses in front of me. I'd never use the word 'lovely' to describe any place, so that doesn't mean anything to me.

"It did. My job is to pull this city back from the unsavory elements trying to destroy it."

Salvo hums excitedly. "A commendable effort! I look forward to celebrating your successes one day. Now, if you'll excuse me, we're preparing for the lunch rush."

"Did you see what happened outside?"

"Unfortunately, no."

"That's not what I heard."

"Oh?"

I have to turn away to hide my smile. Most people in this business are disdainful of the police, and they don't bother to hide it. But Salvo and Giulio get a kick out of feigning respect — as if they know they're on borrowed time and only want to entertain the saints for one more good day before it all comes crashing down. They have the kind of reckless spirit that I appreciate but cannot mimic in the same way, so I keep my mouth shut.

When I look back at Sergeant Gallo, his face is bright red with fury. I can guess what he's thinking, the calculations he's making. If I were him, I would let this go, but he doesn't, and it's my turn to shake my head. I honestly expected better of him.

"Alma," he calls, and our new waitress jumps.

Salvo hired Alma knowing full well that she was an undercover carabinieri, a new recruit courted for exactly this kind of undercover work. I have a contact inside the local precinct, and I'd read her file the day before she'd been sworn in. I could see why they'd chosen her. She is personable but quiet and seems naïve at first glance, but she doesn't miss anything. She has a great memory, which makes her a fantastic waitress and is probably useful for the police as well, I guess. I'm sure she has a great career ahead of her. I doubt anyone will care that she's failed here; she isn't the first one to do so, and it isn't entirely her fault.

"Sir?" Alma says, clutching the pen in her hand. She looks from Salvo to Gallo and then down at the floor.

"Did you see the commotion out front?"

She looks left and right again, probably trying to find any way to salvage her operation.

"It's okay," Salvo says in a gentle voice. "Tell your commander whatever you know."

Gallo and Alma both start at his words. I don't hide my smile this time.

"I-I don't..."

Salvo shakes his head and clucks his tongue like a disappointed mother. "Come now. Lying is so unbecoming." He shrugs. "More lying, I mean."

Alma turns to look at Gallo, hoping for guidance from the man who just trashed three months of her first assignment. I almost feel sorry for her. "I didn't see anything," she finally admits. "I was in the kitchen helping with lunch preparation."

Thanks to me, I think. If Salvo is determined to let these carabinieri send any manner of spies into the restaurant, it's my job to make sure that they stay away from his business as much as possible. That was normally an easier thing to do when Giulio was around, but thankfully, I'd had the where-withal to send her into the kitchen as soon as Salvo had stood from his table, letting our other waitress, Gianna, handle the floor while I told him about the incident at Giuseppe's this morning.

I can't believe that just a few hours ago, I'd thought the shakedown was possibly no big thing; there was always someone biting at our ankles, trying to encroach on our territory. It was just part of the life. But that stronzo in the square, in broad daylight, with a gun aimed at Salvo's head, was a very big thing that we need to handle immediately.

But first, we have to get Gallo out of here.

I want to look at that table, and I almost do. That would have been a dire mistake, especially with Gallo and Alma both desperate for a reason to stay or take Salvo in. But just as I feel my resolve weakening, Giulio bursts through the front door, a box of fresh bread in his hands and a goofy grin on his face. "Boss, did you order more bread?" he asks, looking down at the box and not at the table where Zahra and her sisters are watching him.

I guess they can look wherever they want as tourists, but if it had been up to me, I would have told them to ignore whatever was going on and eat their food. I don't want to give Gallo any reason to look their way.

"No, I didn't."

"Does Giuseppe know that?" Giulio asks.

Salvo looks into the box and then at me. He shrugs. "Ah, well. Who are we to turn down a nice gesture? Alfonso, send a bottle of wine to them, will you?"

I nod and lean over the box. "Are there any pasticcini?" I ask.

"No," Giulio says.

When I try to reach into the box, he swats my hand away.

"I said no."

"You're lying."

Salvo sighs. "Good afternoon, sergeant."

We both turn to Gallo. A vein has appeared, bisecting his forehead, and his jaw is clenched so hard, I'm worry he'll crack a few teeth. I watch him closely. Desperate men are the most dangerous. After a few tense moments, he turns on his heels with a curse. Alma remains, rooted to the spot and looking confused.

Salvo pats her on the shoulder kindly. "You should follow him," he says gently. "Thank you for all your work."

She looks as if she's about to cry as she turns and walks from the restaurant. Giulio and I watch her. "You should reach out to her in a few weeks," I say quietly.

Giulio scoffs. "Obviously. Hopefully, she'll be angry enough to become another mole."

"Probably," I say. "So, are there pasticcini in there or not?"

He grabs the box of bread before he answers, "No."

I reach for it, and he backs away.

"Basta," Salvo says wearily. "Once the carabinieri are gone, clear the restaurant and send the cooks home. I don't want anyone here. If something is happening, it could get dangerous."

"Something *is* happening," I say.

Salvo nods his head gravely.

"What about them?" Giulio asks.

It's as if that question gives us all permission to look at the table with the three women. We find them looking back at us as well.

"Not here," Salvo says in a rough voice. "We need to get them somewhere safe."

"THE AUNTIES ARE GOING to hear about this," I tell Zahra.

Zahra sighs in frustration. "Fine. I get it. I should have just sent an email or texted."

We're walking down a narrow alley between two dark gray apartment buildings that are so damn close together I can't even believe there's a walkway here at all. I look up at the sliver of sky partially occluded by hanging clothes and sheets. I feel like I'm in a shitty alternate universe of my life and not just on another continent.

"Hell, a carrier pigeon would have been good, too," I tell Zahra.

"Next time."

"Next time? Do you plan to run away to another foreign country and shack up with a strange man again?"

"She does not," the dark-haired one calls from behind us.

My sister turns to look around me. She gives him another one of those smiles Ryan never inspired in her. "We'll see."

He says something in Italian that I can guess at by the thick fog of his voice and the way my sister licks her lips at him.

"Gross," I say.

She rolls her eyes at me.

"In here," the big one says, opening a heavy metal door I would have missed.

The gray-haired one — God, I really need to learn these people's names — ushers Shae inside ahead of him and then follows her, their hands clasped together.

"If I had called," Zahra whispers, "we wouldn't have brought those two back together."

"We?" I shriek, before leaning forward to whisper, "And when are we going to talk about whatever the fuck that is?"

"Not now," the big one says, moving his hands to get us inside faster.

"Excuse you," I say.

He lifts his eyebrows and then winks at me.

I roll my eyes in return.

We follow Shae and the gray-haired man into an unassuming apartment building. I can hear someone yelling. They sound like they're cursing someone all the way out behind one door, children are laughing and singing behind another, and the smell of some kind of simmering sauce seems like a really great stereotype, but it makes my stomach rumble all the same.

"I'm hungry," Zahra whines just as I'm wondering if these men will feed us.

"I'll order something," the dark-haired man calls immediately.

"Okay," I concede. "I can see why you stayed."

"Sorry, can you say that louder?" my annoying ass sister practically yells.

"No. And lower your voice."

"Please," the big one says. "We are trying to keep a low profile."

The dark-haired one grunts as if he wants to tell his friend off, even though he's clearly correct. That makes me smile smugly at the back of my sister's head.

"Don't look at me like that," she whines again.

"Maybe we should all stop speaking," the gray-haired one says in a strained voice.

Zahra, the dark-haired one, the big one, and I all glance at one another, chastened. If I wasn't sure who was in charge of this entire operation before, I am now.

We arrive at a door. The gray-haired one lets go of Shae's hand long enough to fish a keyring from his pockets. She turns to look at us, a shy smile on her face.

I see Zahra about to make a very rude gesture with her hands toward our cousin, and I reach around her to grab her wrists. "Please grow up," I whisper.

Shae laughs at us, and the gray-haired man turns to her. I watch him watching her, and just like I've never seen Zahra smile the way she has today at any point in all those years she spent with Ryan, I never saw Steve look at Shae like this. The way she deserves.

"The fuck is in the water here?" I whisper as we follow Shae and her gray-haired baby daddy into this apartment.

"Nothing," the big one whispers, suddenly closer behind me than he was before. "Why? What have you heard?"

I turn to him. He winks at me again.

"Can you stop winking at me, please?"

Zahra bursts into childish giggles.

Alfonso

"Don't look at her like that," Giulio hisses at me.

"Like what?"

"Like *that*," he says. "She's Zahra's sister."

"And?"

He rolls his eyes and nods toward the kitchen table, where Salvo is watching the other woman drink a bottle of water with every ounce of his attention. "Do you know anything about that?"

I shake my head quickly. "Nothing. When did he meet her?"

"No idea."

I turn to him because I need to broach this subject even though I don't want to; it's Giulio's job to be tactful.

"No," he says before I can even open my mouth. Before I even have the words I need. "It's not what you're thinking."

"How do you know what I'm thinking?"

"Because I know you. And you should be thinking what you're thinking, but it's not that."

"How do you know?"

"Hi," Zahra calls from across the room. "Do you two realize that you're shouting?"

When we turn, everyone is staring at us, including Salvo. I catch his eye and think very loudly the words

Giulio didn't allow me to speak. Thankfully, Salvo is more levelheaded.

He pats the woman's hand and then stands slowly from the table. "I think it is time we talked. This is an unexpectedly eventful day."

"Big understatement. Huge," the tall one I can't stop looking at says.

"*Pretty Woman*," Zahra and her other sister say at the same time.

Salvo, Giulio, and I look in confusion at one another.

"Okay," he says tentatively. "Let us start with introductions."

ALFONSO WON'T STOP STARING at me.

Now that I know their names, nothing much changes besides the fact that Alfonso only addresses me by my name while still trying to burn a hole in my bra with his gaze. Giulio is still flirting with Zahra shamelessly, and whatever the fuck is happening between Shae and Salvatore is still very intense.

"Will someone tell me what the fuck is going on?" I cry to no one in particular for what feels like the hundredth time today.

Of course, Alfonso is the only one who registers that I've spoken at all. He looks at me with a bunched brow, but that doesn't answer my question. I roll my eyes and stare at the side of Salvatore's face, hoping that he will feel my gaze boring into his cheek.

He does not.

So, I shift my eyes to Shae. Thankfully, she gets the hint.

Shae turns toward me, and the wistful grin that's been inching onto her face falls. "Huh?" she asks.

I roll my eyes and push up from my chair, and everyone else at the table finally looks in my direction. Alfonso leans back in his seat, the smile on his face widening as he takes me in from head to toe.

"What. The. Fuck. Is going on?" I pose the question again, but this time I wave my hands wildly at the table. "Who the fuck are these dudes?"

Salvatore frowns. "We've introduced ourselves already. Should we do it again?" He aims this question at Shae with a furrowed brow. The subtext of his question — I decide — is to ask her if I'm the dimmest bulb in the box.

Which is offensive, by the way.

I scoff. "I know who you are, but how in the fuck did you meet my cousin, and then a few months later, he," I gesture toward Giulio, "meet my sister? That's a little *too* much of a coincidence for me."

Alfonso jabs Giulio in his side. "Exactly what I wanted to know. I like her."

I ignore him and look at my sister and cousin. They look at the men next to them. I scoff in disgust. Haven't I raised them better than this?

This question only has seconds to form in my mind before I push it away because I absolutely have. I snap my fingers and pull their attention back to me. At least they have the wherewithal to blush in embarrassment. Good. Imagine looking to a man for answers.

"Something's up," I say.

"It's a coincidence," Salvatore says.

"Bullshit," I shoot back at him. I see Shae bristle in my peripheral vision.

That's interesting.

"Shae and I met in late winter. She came here by chance."

Sounds fake, but okay, so I turn to Zahra.

She has the nerve to smile and then shrug. "I met Giulio at my honeymoon hotel," Zahra says in a breezy tone. She actually has the nerve to fucking sigh and sink into her chair while staring deep into his eyes. "I hated him for a few days, and then..." Her voice trails off.

"And then?"

She kisses him instead of answering me. I roll my eyes and turn to my cousin. "Shae?" I'm not really asking her a specific question, so of course, I don't get a useful answer.

"I-I came to Naples when I was in Italy with Steve," she says, her eyes darting nervously toward Salvatore.

"Yes, you already told us that."

"Ugh." Zahra pulls away from Giulio's mouth just long enough to express her annoyance.

"I told you she broke up with him."

"I know. I'm just sayin'," she says and then kisses Giulio's cheek.

I can't look away fast enough. "So, you came to Naples," I prod Shae.

"And I ended up at the restaurant. I found it on Yelp. It had great reviews," she says with a shrug.

"Mariana will love hearing that," Alfonso says.

"It was a coincidence," Shae says.

"Oh, I love that," Zahra says, leaning over Giulio to grab Shae's arm. "I also love that you dumped that dickhead. My

God, he sucked." Giulio laughs and presses a kiss against the side of Zahra's head.

"Yes, yes, yes. Everyone hates Steve. Can we get to the matter at hand? Why the hell did someone try to shoot you?" I ask Salvatore.

"I was wondering when you were going to ask that," he says calmly.

I know he's the boss, but in that moment, I also know that he must be powerful as hell. Only someone in possession of enough clout to take danger for granted could manage to look at me with twinkling eyes behind his glasses and a proud smirk on his face while we discuss an assassination attempt against him.

I turn to Shae and then Zahra. "What the fuck have you two gotten yourselves into?"

Alfonso

Well, that little family drama was a nice interlude. I've spent the last decade enduring my own family's interrogations whenever I made it home, so it's nice to watch someone else have to withstand that kind of scrutiny. It's comforting. My mother and brothers would like Zoe.

But once she aims her attention at Salvo, I know that it's time to get to work.

Giulio and I look to Salvatore, but he only has eyes for Shae.

He's holding her hands in his, and he brings them to his mouth. We all look away from the intimacy of this moment.

Not that I would have expected it, but I can't even remember seeing Salvo touching Flavia like this in all the years they'd been married. And while he's not the kind of man who would hide his humanity, this kind of tenderness is different. Giulio must know that because he pulls Zahra closer into his side and kisses her cheek again.

I turn to Zoe.

She turns to me and frowns.

I raise my eyebrows at her.

Her frown deepens, and she rolls her eyes, looking away.

I laugh.

Salvo's chair scrapes against the floor, and he stands up. "There are things that I cannot tell you, especially not now." He's speaking directly to Shae. They hold a heated — and uncomfortably long — bit of eye contact, and then he turns to us.

"Here's what I can share. I am a businessman with a number of enemies."

"Oh, okay, he's a gangster," Zoe says.

"I mean, I thought so, because Giulio's a bit" — Zahra holds both hands up as if she has a gun in each, and she shoots them — "but I didn't want to judge."

"I guess that explains the room with the dead body," Shae says.

"Uh, he wasn't dead," I add helpfully.

Shae leans forward to whisper to her family members, "See how he used the past tense?"

I look toward Salvo and Giulio. My boss looks bewildered.

Giulio shrugs and hugs Zahra. "She was bound to figure it out eventually."

"I mean, I assumed when you," she shoots her finger guns again, "in San Gimignano." She turns to Salvo. "Okay, so you're a 'businessman,'" she makes quotation marks with her fingers, "with a lot of enemies."

Salvo's mouth falls open. "I..." His brow furrows, and he curses in Italian.

My phone rings, and I answer it as Salvo collects himself and begins to speak. I don't need to hear this. I know what kind of man I am.

"Ciao."

"Alfonso," the voice says. I recognize Tommaso's thick Sicilian accent.

"Si."

"We have a problem."

"No," I say. "We cannot."

I can hear the shrug in his voice. "And yet we do. Do you want to hear it, or would you prefer to waste more time living in denial? I can call you later if you would like."

"Alright," I say, shaking my fist at the air even though he's not here to see it. "Tell me."

"Someone broke into my home yesterday," he says in an affronted voice.

"What a disgrace," I say. "What is the world coming to?"

"I haven't the faintest idea, my friend. But I just wanted to let you know that someone tried to steal that antique armoire you gave me. I would have been devastated if they'd taken such an important gift."

I grunt, my mind already working, pulling all of these pieces together.

"I used to think my home was the safest place on earth, but I'm beginning to believe that I was wrong."

I grunt again. "That really is a shame. I'm sorry to hear that. I'll understand if you need to return the gift."

"I hope it won't come to that, but it's an avenue we should explore."

"Let me consider the options for transportation, and I'll contact you."

"Of course. I'll wait for your call."

I nod and hang up. I am not the brains of this operation — I would never want to be — but even I can see that *something* is happening, and if we don't act now, it could turn into something very dangerous.

WHEN I WALK BACK into the living room, Salvo is standing behind Shae's chair, one hand on her shoulder and the other running through his hair.

"Salvo." Everyone turns to me, but I focus on him. "We need to speak."

"We're listening," Zoe responds. She's sexy but not *that* sexy. I nod my head toward the bedroom and give Giulio a meaningful look to communicate that he should join us.

"Rude," Zoe says, as Giulio's chair scrapes and Salvo whispers to Shae that he won't be gone long.

"Only you would think to antagonize the big bruiser," Shae says.

"I think I can take him," Zoe replies.

And I can't help it. I turn toward her with a smile on my face. "Anytime," I tell her. "All you have to do is ask."

She rolls her eyes and bites back a smile.

"Who called you?" Salvo asks as soon as the bedroom door is closed.

I tell him quickly about Tommaso's phone call.

As I speak, Giulio becomes agitated. "They're making a move," he says.

"And who exactly is 'they'?" Salvo asks. "That's the only thing that matters."

"Is it Flavia's family? Again?" Giulio asks.

Salvo shakes his head, but he doesn't answer.

"While you've been on your honeymoon, I've been working." I don't need to elaborate.

"Without me?" he looks offended.

I roll my eyes and brush those words away.

"Still," he says. "You could have invited me." He actually sounds offended.

"It's not Flavia's family," Salvo says, getting us back on track.

"Could it be the Ginetti family?"

"Of course. It could be any of my enemies. It could be any of my allies."

"But why go after Flavia?" I ask.

Giulio and I wait while he considers the question. He walks around the room, his hands behind his back. This is his thinking pose. While Salvo is a normally patient man, I once saw him break someone's nose for interrupting him while he was deep in thought. It's been years, but it's the kind of thing that you only need to see once to learn a lesson. Even for me.

"If I were making this move," Salvo eventually says, "I'd go after Flavia for one of two reasons. One, if I wanted to cripple me; or two, if I wanted to legitimize myself."

"Didn't you marry her to legitimize yourself?" Giulio asks.

Salvo scoffs. "Hopefully, whoever is coming for me learned from my mistake."

"So, you think it's the first one?" I ask.

"I think I don't know enough to be sure, but I know who will." He turns to me. "Call Tommaso. Tell him I'm coming for a visit."

I nod, already reaching for my phone.

"I'll watch over Shae while you're away," Giulio says seriously.

Salvo shakes his head. "She comes with me." His voice is so hard that it sucks the air out of the room with a crackling tension. Giulio takes an unconscious step back.

My fingers stop moving over my phone screen. "I...don't know how the other women will react to that," I say carefully.

Salvo smiles. "I imagine that they will put up a fight."

"Zahra seems very meek, but that's just a façade," Giulio says.

Salvo and I stare at him. "If you think Zahra seems meek, then love is clouding your vision much more seriously than I thought," Salvo says, with more tact than I could have managed.

"Your head is too far up her pussy if you think she's meek," I agree.

Giulio smiles and shrugs. "It is a great place to be. You should try it sometime."

"Later," Salvo says. He takes a deep breath before opening the door.

Zoe

"Yeah, that's not going to happen," I say. "I'm not letting you take my cousin halfway across the country."

"She'll be safe with me," Salvatore says.

"Oh, I believe that. One hundred percent. Whatever this is, is very adorable, actually. But we were sent here to get this one—" I point at my sister.

"I have a name," she says childishly.

I ignore her. "—and return home. Whatever gang war is brewing here seems dangerous. That sucks for y'all. I'll take these two home and get back to my life. Hope it works out for everyone in the end."

"Um, I'm not going home," Zahra says.

"What?" Shae and I screech.

Zahra's eyes are wide. "I don't mean like ever. Chill. I just mean like right now. I'm staying here with Giulio." He's beaming at her words. "Don't get cocky," she tells him.

"Of course not," he laughs.

"Hello, have you missed the whole gang war thing happening around us? No sex is good enough for that," I say.

Giulio turns to me and winks. "You might be surprised."

I snap my fingers at him, and he frowns. "Tighten up, Romeo. We're talking about important shit here."

Alfonso doubles over in laughter behind me.

I turn to my cousin. "Shae, you don't have to go with him. You know that, right?"

She looks at me with big, blinking eyes that begin to water. "I know," she says.

"Of course, she doesn't," Salvatore says.

She turns to him. "It is not a bad idea," he concedes, "for you to leave the country. You would be safer as far as away from me as you can get. And I will not lie; I would be happier knowing that you were safe. It would make everything easier. And you deserve to have a better life than running from danger with me."

"Shut up!" she screams, pushing away from him and standing abruptly. She's speaking to Salvatore, but I think everyone in the room freezes.

I look at Zahra with wide eyes and make eye contact with my sister. I know we're both thinking the same thing. If this goes left, I'll hit the big one over the head with my chair or something, and she can use Giulio's feelings for her to incapacitate him in some way. The three of us can maybe take Salvatore on, and then we'll just have to run for our lives. Or something.

"You said that before, that I deserved better. That I should go back to my life, but my life fucking sucks. My boyfriend—"

"Ex-boyfriend," Zahra and I add helpfully.

Shae glares at us.

"Sorry," Zahra mumbles.

"Just sayin'," I whisper under my breath.

"My *ex*-boyfriend fucking sucked. I went back to my life, and all I could think about was you. Even when I didn't want to. Even when all I wanted to remember about you was you saying goodbye, life had other plans."

"Bella," Salvatore says, standing and reaching for her. "Listen."

She pushes his hands away. "No, you listen. You don't get to push me away or send me back to the States for my own good again. We did that. I hated it. I'm staying with you."

"Hold on," I say.

"Love this," Zahra says.

"I'm pregnant!" Shae yells at the top of her lungs. "And I'm staying with my baby's daddy."

The entire room goes still and quiet again. Except for me. I groan as loud as I can.

The Council is going to be so pissed.

I look left and right, making eye contact with everyone except Shae and Salvatore because they're only looking at one another. Zahra, Alfonso, Giulio, and I are shocked. None of this is going the way I expected on the flight over. This is far more complicated than the Aunties thought it would be.

I sigh, knowing that I'll have to send them a message soon explaining why this wasn't a quick return trip, and I have no fucking idea how I'll make sense of all this. And apparently, now I can't even ask Shae for help.

"This is the worst fucking daytime soap ever," I mumble.

"Worst or best?" Alfonso whispers to me. "I would watch this faithfully."

I turn to him and frown. He smiles in return. I snap in his face, but unlike Giulio, he seems to enjoy it.

Alfonso and I turn at the sound of Salvatore's voice. "Then it's settled," he says in a thick voice that even makes me shudder. "You will come with me. We have a lot to consider."

"Oh, good," Alfonso says. "What do you want us to do?"

Giulio waves his hand and scoffs in annoyance.

Alfonso shrugs. "This is my job. Your job as well."

"He's right," Salvatore says.

"I don't think it is a good idea for us to be together. We need to know who's coming after you, but we don't need to make it easy for them to take us all out at once. That's what I would do."

Zahra and I look at one another. Her eyes are wide, but I'm squinting at her because what the fuck has she gotten us all into?

"My bad," she mouths. "I think I love him."

I roll my eyes.

Salvatore takes a few seconds of quiet to think. He shoves one hand into his pants pocket, but the other flattens against Shae's stomach. I see my cousin's bottom lip quiver and her eyes water when she looks at him. I look back at Zahra.

"Awww," she mouths.

"It's cute," I mouth back. I'm not heartless.

"Shae and I will go south," Salvatore says. "Giulio will stay here with Zahra." My sister squeaks and throws her arms around Giulio's shoulders.

"Gag," I say, and Alfonso chuckles.

Salvatore turns to us. "Alfonso, you should leave as well."

He nods. "I shouldn't go far."

Salvatore agrees. "I'm sorry to ask this of you," he says

with surprisingly kind eyes. "I imagine this might get complicated."

It's strange, but in that moment, I can see what Shae might have seen in him.

Alfonso shrugs. "It's fine. My mother will be so happy that she'll feed me well, at least."

Salvatore smiles. "Take her," he says, nodding toward me.

"Excuse me?" I shriek.

Salvatore looks at me. "Whoever is after me saw you this morning. You three are hard to miss."

"We have great genes," Zahra says.

"The best," Alfonso agrees, leaning toward me.

I cut my eyes at him.

"It would be a good thing not to keep you in the city."

"And Zahra's staying." Giulio raises his hands. "I'll shoot anyone who ruins her mood. She'll be very safe with me." My sister preens at his terrifying pledge.

"Is it the water? Is that what has you two acting like this?"

"I hope so," Alfonso says, "considering where we are going."

"I'm not going with you," I say. "I have a life. A job. A bunch of old Black women who are waiting for me to get these two back."

Salvatore squints in confusion. "I can have Alfonso take you to the airport. We can send you home," he says. "Alone."

"I—" My gaze shifts to Shae, and I can see in her face that Salvatore isn't lying. If I leave now, it won't be with her. I don't even need to look at my sister to know she'll be looking at me with the same conviction. I nod at Salvatore. "I'm not leaving this country without these two."

He nods. "You are incredibly loyal. So are we. Nothing will happen to them, and Alfonso will protect you as surely as Giulio and I will protect Zahra and Shae. After that, you are welcome to try and convince them to return. I promise that we will handle this matter as quickly as possible."

"This matter," I mumble and then turn to Alfonso.

"I hope you brought comfortable shoes," he says ominously.

"No," I tell Alfonso for the third time since we got off the boat at the makeshift harbor in Positano.

I feel as if the past five hours have been some kind of beautiful nightmare; absolutely fantastic views but a horrible plot. I want to wake up, or at least start over now that I'm semi-conscious. I want a chance to change things, starting with this steep ass set of stone steps winding up the side of this mountain.

"I refuse," I tell Alfonso.

He laughs, but he doesn't stop trudging up, up, up.

"Why can't we stay somewhere down here?" I whine.

"There's nothing down here besides the beach, restaurants, and shops. Even the hotels are up in the mountain."

"Why? How? Why would someone do this?"

Alfonso shrugs. "It's just how it is and how it's always been."

"There's no elevator?"

"Not to where we're going." He turns around and stops walking.

I stop walking as well and huff, trying to get more air into my lungs than might actually exist in this place.

"There's another way," he says.

"Finally."

"Some people use donkeys," he begins to say.

"Fuck you," I wheeze and begin to walk, bumping into his arm. But he's so goddamn big and solid that I'm the one knocked unsteady on my feet. His hand wraps around my waist unexpectedly to steady me, and I jolt, jumping from his grip.

He laughs and presses me forward, following close behind, huffing as well. "You should pace yourself," he says. "Two hundred and fifty steps is a lot to handle, especially the first time."

My feet stop, and I turn to him. "How many?!" I scream. I ignore the people stopping to stare at me. I don't care what anyone thinks right now because I'm already so goddamn tired.

"Don't worry," he says, patting me on the small of my back. "The first time is always the worst, but after that's, it's a breeze."

"You're a terrible liar," I tell him.

He smiles. "I am. That's why I'm the muscle."

My legs are on fire. My chest feels like it's full of nothing but stitches. Hell, even my ass hurts. I wince as I collapse onto the low stone wall standing between the steps and a steep cliff.

"I hate you," I pant.

We've made it to wherever the fuck Alfonso is going to stash me away from the gang war brewing in Naples. I'm so winded that for the first time, I'm not thinking about my sister being in the middle of all that probable danger or the fact that Salvo is taking Shae somewhere so private that they don't even tell us the exact location. Just in case. I'm so tired that I can't even worry about what the Aunties will think about all this mess. I'm so tired that I would prefer to return to the nightmare I thought I was living in at the bottom of the mountain. Before I knew exactly how much pain two hundred and fifty steps could inflict on my body.

"That's okay. You made it, and that's all that matters. I'm proud of you." He's deposited our bags at the front of this large wooden door set into the mountain.

If I were less exhausted, I would marvel at how beautiful the scenery is. If I didn't feel as if one of my lungs was on the verge of collapse, I might even find the breath to thank him for carrying my suitcase and his bags up the steps as well. But I'm close to death's door — I swear it — and I don't have time for good manners.

"I hope you die." It actually hurts to say those words, so chances are high that I'll die before he does, but a girl can dream.

As usual, he laughs. "You might be the most beautiful person to ever wish death on me. I'm going to take that as a compliment." He straightens up and pulls a key on a long chain from his bag, and unlocks the beautiful wooden door. "Can you walk a few more meters?"

I don't know what I hate most; the adorably boyish smile on his face, the gentle tenor of his voice, or myself because I actually like both of those things.

"As soon as I can feel my legs again, you better feed me," I tell him.

"Of course I will," he says, offering me his hand.

I groan loudly as he pulls me up from the wall. And even though I don't want to encourage this kind of casual and familiar touching, I do appreciate his arm around my waist as I limp into something that looks like a gorgeous jungle.

"Are you kidding me?" I gasp. "This is beautiful."

"You seem shocked," Alfonso says.

"Obviously, I am. I thought you were going to take me to hide in some dark warehouse somewhere."

He chuckles. "I don't think Zahra would appreciate that," he says. "And I wouldn't like to fight with Giulio because I made her frown."

I peer up at him. "Would he do that?"

"Hmm?" he asks, at this point practically dragging me toward the house ahead of us.

"Would Giulio fight you because of me?"

"Because of you via Zahra, yes."

"He loves her that much?"

Alfonso smiles. "I don't know that they have used those words, but yes," he laughs. "He loves her that much. I've never seen him like this before. I quite like it, actually. It's much easier to aggravate him."

"So, you like playing with danger," I say, and he freezes. "What?"

His formerly bright face has darkened into a scowl, and suddenly, I'm worried about the same arm around my waist that had been so comforting a few moments ago. I start to push away from him — I don't think I have the strength to run, but I will absolutely try — and his hold tightens around me. Whatever the hell is happening in this moment is thankfully interrupted by someone yelling at us in Italian.

I watch as Alfonso's face brightens again.

I turn to look toward the house and see a man that is absolutely related to Alfonso. He's at least six feet away, and the light under the trellis is dim, deepening the early evening darkness, but I can see the family resemblance in the broad shoulders and thick waist.

Alfonso calls back to him, their Italian blending together musically, their excitement palpable. He begins to drag me forward again. I try to push away, but his hold is tighter than ever.

I don't understand what they're saying, but I know the moment their conversation turns to me. The other man's eyes shift my way, and Alfonso manages to somehow hold me even closer as he says something in a warning tone. And that's when I decide I've had enough.

I give a great shove and finally break Alfonso's hold on me. I don't even care if he let me loose so long as I am. Sure, I'm unsteady as hell on my feet, but that's beside the point.

"English," I tell Alfonso. "If you're going to talk about me like I'm not here, the least you can do is speak in English, so I know just how much to hate you."

A shocked smile spreads across his face, and the other man laughs, but when he begins to speak in Italian, Alfonso cuts him off. "You heard her. English," he says, still looking at me.

There's a teasing laughter in the other man's voice. "I should have known this was the kind of woman you would bring home. Good. You need someone to keep you in line. When are you going to introduce us?" he asks.

Alfonso finally looks away. "Only when you promise not to flirt with her."

He grins. "Oh, unfortunately, I cannot promise that." He looks at me out of the corner of his eye and winks.

Yeah, they're definitely related.

"Zoe," Alfonso says, "this is one of my brothers, Nicola."

"One of?"

"Yes, but he's the worst, so if you manage not to kill him tonight, the other two will be much easier to handle."

"If," Nicola says. "Does mamma know you're back?"

Alfonso shakes his head. "If I'd told her, she'd have met me at the pier."

Nicola's laugh booms across the garden. "She might have come to Naples to fetch you herself."

"I wanted to give Zoe a night to recover. The steps..."

Nicola turns to me with a sympathetic smile. "The first time is the worst," he says. "That's true of the steps and..."

"Basta," Alfonso groans.

Nicola laughs. "Come," he says. "Take her inside. I will get your bags."

"Grazie." Alfonso reaches for me again. "Andiamo."

My mama raised me not to be too proud to accept help. To be honest, that was always a lesson I tried to ignore. But I have maybe one or two good minutes left of standing on my own two feet before I keel over, so against my better judgment, I reach out a hand to Alfonso, and he practically lifts me against his side and carries me down the path.

He calls to Nicola in Italian before leading me away from the main house toward another flight of steps hidden against the side of the building. I groan. He laughs and then gives up the pretense of helping me stand.

I'm pretty sure the last person I willingly let pick me up was my daddy when I was like eight years old. The last man who tried to pick me up without my consent expected me to take it. He didn't plan that my big and tall ass would fight him. I hit him over the head, and we toppled over. I landed on the relative cushion of his skinny ass stomach. I gave him a knot on his head the size of a golf ball. He learned to keep his hands to himself, and everyone in the university food court that day learned not to try me.

I want to teach Alfonso that lesson, but his hold on me is much more secure than that college asshole's had been. Not that I plan to write a sonnet about his thick ass arms or anything. But I'm also so damn tired! For once in my life, when I hear my mother's voice in my head telling me to let someone do something for me, I listen.

Alfonso carries me up the steps to another house, above the first, tucked closer to the mountain. I think he'll let me down at the top of the staircase, but he carries me to the front door. He sets me gently on my feet and makes sure that I'm steady before he pulls that keyring from his pocket and unlocks the door.

"Who does your brother think I am?"

Alfonso blinks at me and blushes. "My fiancée."

"Seriously?" I groan.

"We need a cover story," he says.

"Were there no other options?"

He laughs. "Maybe. Welcome home, amore."

I HAVEN'T BEEN HOME in just over a year. I usually try not to be away for so long — I've let my mother down enough — but the past year has been hectic. The first assassination attempt on Salvo had been a constant thorn in my side, and the last thing I wanted to do was bring that danger to my family's doorsteps.

That's what I tell Salvo, Giulio, and myself. It's not a lie, but it's not the full truth, either.

I don't bother lying to my family, so I say nothing at all, and I've been staying away longer than I should.

Disappointment is a funny thing.

I've been letting my parents down for most of my life. I was sent home from school for fighting. I was sent home from church for stealing cigarettes from the priests. And I was run off of the beach at sixteen by Signora Costa when she caught me and that French girl on holiday with her family getting to know one another. What my parents wanted was four well-behaved boys. What they got was three... No, two good boys and Nicola and me. But at least

Nicola has a respectable job, and he hasn't moved far away from home and his aging parents like I have.

None of us has gotten married and given our mother grandchildren, which is the only thing she says she ever asked of us. I would beg to differ, but I'm never home long enough to engage that debate.

My entire life has been spent with my parents' love and disappointment blanketing me, but each time I come home, what I find unbearable is my disappointment in myself. So, even though she doesn't want to be here, I appreciate that focusing on Zoe allows me some space. Every minute I spend with her means that's one minute when I'm not consumed by everything I've ever done wrong in my entire life.

This house was supposed to be mine. The plan had always been to shuffle us around these plots of land that my family has owned longer than anyone could rightly remember. Once I got married and had children, my mother had expected me to move here so she would be nearby. Instead, I moved to Naples. Each time I return to this house and this life that I've left, the certainty I feel about my life falters. But I don't have the privilege to let that happen this time.

"You can have this bathroom to yourself," I tell her. "And this room here. There should be some fresh sheets and towels downstairs at Nicola's."

"Did someone call my name?" Nicola sings as he huffs into the house.

"No," I yell back.

"Maybe next time." He rolls Zoe's suitcase into view. "Or maybe my French is better than my English, yes?"

"Stop."

He ignores me and winks at Zoe.

"When was the last time you changed the sheets up here?" I ask irritably.

He laughs. "Just last week," he says, sounding offended. "Dario wanted to spend a weekend away from the rectory."

"Rectory?"

"Our youngest brother is a priest," I tell her. "Our mother's favorite."

Nicola makes a strange guttural noise, and I cut my eyes in his direction. "Do you have anything to eat?"

"Of course, I do," he says. "Gli avanzi di mamma." He frowns in Zoe's direction. "I need a wife to cook for me."

I crack my knuckles, and Nicola backs away, doubling over in laughter.

"Well, good luck finding her," Zoe says. "I don't cook or clean for myself, so I'm damn sure not doing it for a man."

Nicola's laughter rises. "Capisco! She's perfect for you."

Zoe sighs. "Can I shower? Alone?" she says. "My entire body hurts."

"Oh, then you should give your fiancée a massage, Alfonso. You're a better man than this."

"I—"

"No, thanks," Zoe cuts in. "You can take him down with you. I'd love to try your mother's cooking once I've showered." She smiles solicitously at me, nothing like a fiancée or a girlfriend but like a woman who is very used to getting men to do her bidding because she knows how beautiful she is.

She doesn't need to bat her eyelashes at me, however. It's my job to keep her safe and comfortable.

"Va bene, carina," I say, trying to sound as if this is a

thing I have said to her hundreds of times before. I lean down awkwardly to brush my mouth against her cheek in a simulation of a kiss.

And my brother, the child that he is, whistles under his breath and says something rude that Zoe thankfully cannot understand.

But it's easy to ignore him as I sink my fingers into her soft waist, and she inhales on a sharp moan.

Before we leave, Nicola and I open the windows to let some cool air into the house. I stash my duffel bag in the bedroom on the other side of the kitchen.

Outside, Nicola is laughing at his phone.

"What's funny?" I ask.

He smiles up at me. "Ugo sent me a message telling me that he heard you were in town."

I groan. "How? We came directly here from the ferry."

He claps me on my shoulder. "You've been gone too long, fratello. You've forgotten how small Positano really is. Mamma probably knows that you're here already."

I shake my head. "She can't."

Nicola laughs. "She can."

I glance back at the house, but Nicola pulls me away. "She'll be fine. I think mamma will like her."

I roll my eyes in annoyance. "You're just saying that."

He laughs louder. "I am! Come. You can take whatever food you want from my house before I leave."

"Where are you going?"

"I have a charter to Sorrento tonight. I'll stay there and

be back tomorrow. I hope I don't miss when Zoe meets mamma."

We jog down the steps. "I forgot how annoying you can be."

"And this is one of the many reasons why you need to come home more often," he laughs, but this peal of laughter sounds slightly hollower than all the others.

A HOT SHOWER will fix most things.

This is the kind of self-care advice my mother gave me as a stressed-out teenager, and she was usually right.

Unfortunately, the water in the bathroom only ever gets to slightly above lukewarm. I might have been okay with that but for the tiny ass shower stall that reminds me of transportation pods on spaceships in movies. Maybe Italian showers are where they got the idea. I always thought I would feel claustrophobic in them as a kid, and twenty-something years later, I know that I'm right. That's some comfort, at least, but not much.

I have to deal with the indignity of wrapping a plastic bag over my head to protect my hair from the showerhead that pours directly into the stall. And I cringe every time my body slides along the shower walls. I don't want to seem ungrateful — my parents raised me better than that — but if this is how this little mob vacay is starting, I don't know how long I'm gonna last.

I didn't even want to agree to this whole hide-out situation. I thought I could suck it up because, honestly, it seemed better than returning to the Council of Aunties and being grilled on how not one but now two women in our family are currently MIA in Italy. But if this little jaunt into a bad chick-lit film adaptation keeps going downhill like this, I might have to consider calling in reinforcements.

Maybe I need to get the big guns, aka Auntie Mabel. The thought makes me shudder right around when the warm water gives out.

I sigh at my wholly unsatisfactory shower and step out into the bathroom and realize that there's just one more indignity I need to endure. There's a tall cabinet at the corner of the room, and I open it to find it surprisingly stacked with towels that smell like detergent and sun. I smile right up until I pull the largest one out and realize that I *might* be able to get this thing around one thigh, but that's about it.

My mouth falls open in shock, but then I have to shake my head because what did I really expect after that claustrophobic ass shower?

I use the towel to dry my body and then go through my regular skin and body care routine. I might not feel like myself, but I can at least smell like my favorite melon body butter and take comfort in doing my full five-step skincare routine. It's the little self-care things.

I step back and look at myself in the small well-lit mirror behind the pedestal sink. Well, what I can see of my body, which is mostly just from the tip of my chin to the bottom curve of my stomach, which hides the top of my mound.

Looking at myself puts a smile on my face. Some might call it vanity, but I believe in loving myself first.

I turn to the side and enjoy the profile.

I don't ever plan to have kids, so the advice I always gave Zahra and Shae and will one day pass onto their children—

Oh my God, Shae's pregnant!

I remember that in a rush of shock that saps me of every bit of reserve energy I have left. I decide to fret about that later, after I've eaten and had a good night's sleep. Anyway, the advice I plan to give to my nieces and nephews includes that one should never miss an opportunity to take a good but tasteful nude.

Thankfully, unlike most of my mother's advice, I always follow my own.

I reach for my phone and take a burst of my body from as many angles as possible. The fact that this mirror cuts off my face is ideal; I hate having to edit *every single picture* to obscure my face before I send it out.

Oh, but then thinking that makes me sad. For the past two years, I've had a regular place to send my nudes. I didn't have to wonder what Tyrone or Kevin would think of my body or pictures because I knew they loved them. They loved them so much that they'd sometimes project them onto the wall of their bedroom so we could all admire me while we fucked.

I've managed not to think about my exes for a few hours — because of all the drama — but now that I have, I feel like the world is crumbling underneath my feet. I don't even look at the obviously spectacular images I've taken. I don't have the heart.

I throw the too-small towel over the shower door to air dry and decide to walk to my bedroom alone.

I forgot about Alfonso.

Alfonso

"Mi raccomando, calpestami."

I'm not hard up for a woman; never have been. But Jesus Christ, I've never met a woman like Zoe. It's not just the way her thighs and stomach jiggle as she walks, the way her soft brown nipples harden in the cool air, or the fact that when she realizes that I'm standing in the kitchen, arms full of containers of my mother's cooking, including some pasticcini, and a cloth bag with fresh bread dangling from my lips, she freezes, turns to me, and smiles.

"Oh good, I'm starving," she breathes. "Give me a second."

That's it.

There's no shocked gasp or desperate attempt to hide all that beauty with her hands. Just stuttering steps as she realizes she's not alone, a small grin, and then a slow glide into her bedroom.

"Dio mio," I whisper when she's gone.

I begin to reheat the various dishes Nicola shoved into my hands, but it's as if someone else is controlling the movement of my limbs. Someone else uncovers each dish. Someone else decides which dishes should be cold or hot. Someone else slices the loaf of bread. Someone else searches in the kitchen drawers for a grater for the block of parmesan Nicola shoved into an empty space in my overloaded arms. Someone else prepares Zoe's dinner because I'm too preoccupied remembering every curve of her body while also, futilely, trying to will my cock to deflate.

Zoe

Okay, this trip is a whole mess.

My younger sister and cousin are dickmatized.

The shower was unsatisfying.

And my love life is a mess.

But holy fuck, this is the best roast chicken I've ever had in my life.

"Are you going to eat that?" I ask, pointing toward the bit of breast meat left in the dish.

Alfonso shakes his head and pushes the plate toward me.

I spear the meat greedily. "Your mother is amazing. Holy shit."

That brings a small smile to his face, and he moves another dish of new potatoes, onions, and capers toward me, so I dish some of that onto my plate as well.

"Is she a chef? Does your family own a restaurant?"

"No. She'll be happy to hear that you think so highly of her cooking."

"I do. I really, really do."

"Wait until you taste her cake."

I moan. Like tongue on my clit, and another on my asshole, and I'm so close to coming that heaven and hell feel real *moan*.

"Okay, this is the best part of being in hiding. I love it. I promise not to complain for the rest of the night."

Ever since I came out for dinner, Alfonso has seemed muted, as if he was walking through fog. I'm not oblivious; I've rendered many men speechless with my body before. It is a gift.

But apparently, my enthusiasm finally pulls him out of his stupor.

While I shovel a small mound of green beans onto my plate, Alfonso stands from the table to find a knife.

"Wonderful," I mutter happily.

Once again, Alfonso has to help me to my feet and practically carry me. Thank God we don't have to scale dozens of steps this time. Unfortunately, we have other hurdles to tackle, separately and together.

If I liked the feel of his arm around my waist after climbing two hundred and fifty stairs, I love it now after I've eaten his mother's good food and had a couple of glasses of red wine. I am in Italy, you know? This is expected, isn't it?

The mistake I've made — the second mistake? — is being so tired that I forget how horny a couple glasses of wine can make me. It's almost embarrassing, to be honest. My friends can hold out for a couple of cocktails, a shot of something strong and brown, some real top-shelf shit. Me? My basic ass? Nah. All I need is a few good ounces of fermented grapes — don't even have to be good quality wine — and then me and my erogenous zones are ready to have a real conversation with any and every penis in a three-foot radius.

And I do mean every.

"You smell good," I mumble against Alfonso's neck.

"That's the food and wine talking," he laughs.

"Don't mean they're lying," I giggle. I *never* giggle.

He lowers me to the bed and mutters something in a strangled Italian. "I'll bring you some water," he says in English before rushing away.

I fall back onto the bed. It's hard but not uncomfortable. I'm precious about my bathrooms, but not mattresses, apparently. Alfonso is back before I can blink. He places a tall glass of water onto the bedside table. I groan when I feel his hands; one on my thigh, one on the thin blanket under me.

He tucks me in.

"Can you get me something else?" I whine.

"Of course. Anything."

Those three words make my already wet pussy shudder. "In my suitcase," I say. "There's a gray cloth bag on the right-hand side."

He nods quickly and moves to the foot of my bed.

I hear him rummaging in my bag. I hear when he finds what I've sent him to get, and he realizes what it is.

"Merda," he hisses.

I moan.

He groans.

I hear him walk back around the bed to stand beside me, his steps much less hurried.

"Is this what you wanted?" he asks, the familiar rough

virgin cotton of the bag I use to transport my travel toys against my fingers.

I grab onto it and feel the blunt, spongy tip of a toy I plan to wear out sooner than later. And yet, Alfonso asks me that question in a deeper voice than I've heard from him before. It's deep enough to make my already pulsing pussy throb.

"Is this what you need?"

Oh. The way he asks that question is delicious, and if I'd had another glass of wine, I might have taken him up on the offer in his tone.

But I'm not *that* drunk. I pull the bag from his hand. "Close the door when you leave, please."

He's silent for a few seconds, and then he grunts.

My clit jumps at that sound. I'm almost sad when he turns around and walks from the room, closing the door quietly behind him.

THE SHOWER DOESN'T MAKE me feel like myself. Dinner was good, but it didn't soothe my aching muscles. The wine was good but not life-changing.

But as soon as I hear that familiar, comforting hum of my favorite clitoral sucking toy, I feel like myself for the first time since I arrived in Naples. I haven't even touched the toy to my body or slipped my hand underneath my t-shirt to caress my breasts, but I'm already sighing. I pull the waistband of my sleep shorts away from my stomach and slip my right hand between my legs. I use my thumb to change the settings and circle my mound with the toy, just appreciating the feeling of vibrations against my body.

For some people, masturbation is a means to an end, a way to get off quickly, to orgasm as a pressure valve relief. I never leave home without a very small, very powerful bullet for hectic, stressful days, where all I need is ten minutes in an empty bathroom to come quick and hard, and then I'm ready to get back to the rest of my regularly scheduled life.

But that's not how I prefer to masturbate.

My pleasure should be a production. It deserves care, attention, and planning. I take getting myself off seriously, and I don't accept less care and attention from any of my partners. That's yet another thing I'm going to miss most about my exes. The only people as serious about me getting off in whichever way I needed was them, and I loved being with people who allowed me to reciprocate that care.

After the breakup, an international flight, an aborted shooting, and an escape along the coast, I need my vibrator to take my mind off of everything more than ever. I thumb my vibrator settings again and move the head over my clit. That jolts my mind and body into the here and now. I shiver and groan. I press the toy against my clit and my head into the pillow. I shove my left hand under my t-shirt and pinch my nipple. The ripples of that sharp pain radiate out through my body.

I haven't even come yet, but my limbs are feeling looser, my eyes are drooping, and my lips are wet with my arousal.

I won't last long.

Normally, I would feel sad about a quick come. Like I said, my pleasure should be a production, but sometimes the production is having a quiet dinner of amazing leftovers with a big, silent man who makes sure I eat first and subtly spoons more of the dishes I enjoy onto my plate. Sometimes, the thing that makes me wet enough to easily push two fingers into my cunt is being carried to bed by a man who supports my weight easily and seems to enjoy holding me in his big, rough, capable hands. Sometimes, it's just being tucked under the sheets because my recent breakup left me feeling hollow to my core, and I haven't had any time to process my sadness. Sometimes, the care and attention I need is having someone whose gaze I can feel even in a dark bedroom hand me a bag of my favorite toys.

And maybe if I was less physically and emotionally tired, I'd have pulled Alfonso into the bed with me and taught him how to use my favorite toys on me. Maybe, if things weren't so strange, I would have invited Alfonso to help me forget all the chaos for the rest of the night.

Alfonso

If I were a worse man, I would have crouched outside her door. Apparently, the nuns were wrong about me, and I'm not as bad as they said and I came to believe.

I don't go far, though.

Someone has to clear the kitchen table and put up the rest of the food and wash the dishes. Someone has to make sure that the front door and windows are locked. And so, I do that. I also pull out my phone and check in with Giulio and Salvo.

It's a good sign that Giulio responds quickly to my message. I'd expected him to happily barricade himself in his apartment with Zahra and ride out the storm of whatever the fuck is coming between her legs. Maybe that's the plan for later, but tonight, he surprises me when he sends a picture of him and Zahra in Piazza Garibaldi, small cups of gelato in their hands.

He tells me to show the picture to Zoe and to enjoy our vacation. I nod, looking up at the door, remembering all her softness in my arms. I could go knock on her door, beg to be let inside, and crouch by the bed to show her this picture, and then, maybe, I could ask her again if she wanted the toys or if there was something else — someone else — I could offer.

Thankfully, Giulio sends another message and stops me from making that particular mistake.

"While you are in Positano, make sure to swim in the sea. You need to gain some perspective."

I send him a rude emoji in response just as Salvo's message arrives.

"Enjoy the sea and remember that the things that seem most important sometimes lie."

Whatever that means. Maybe I'll ask Giulio tomorrow.

I finally decide that it's time to go to bed. It's been a long day, and now that my mother certainly knows that I'm back home, tomorrow will be even longer. I shut the lights off and turn toward my bedroom. That's as far as I get.

It's as if my hearing improves in the dark.

There are parts of Naples that never sleep — that never get dark enough to hide a couple of teenage boys sneaking out of the house at night to go party on a secluded beach, where the darkness is somehow deeper than it should be but never quite complete. But the quiet up here is a living thing, full of the sounds of living beings — insects, neighbors toasting one another in the night, cries, boat horns on the seas. A large city like Naples can't replicate it, and sometimes, I miss these sounds while I'm away.

But the quiet is shocking now, maybe because Zoe's here, maybe because I can still feel that cloth bag in my hand and guess what she's doing. I feel wide awake. And with the lights off, I can hear the soft electric hum coming from her room, and my resolve to go to bed disappears.

I'm rooted to this spot in the kitchen, one hand on the light switch, the other holding my mobile phone in a death grip. I want to move closer. Once again, I consider walking back to her door. I know I'm not as bad a man as I imagine, but I wish I was. I wish I could throw her door open. I think about it. I want it.

But this floor is old, and it creaks. I'm terrified that the hum will cease at my first step.

So, I stand there and listen to that hum, desperate for more, and Zoe gives it to me.

Her soft moan is too polite. It's contained and muffled as if she's worried that I might hear, and that undoes me.

The possibility that she's touching herself and thinking about me in any way makes the erection I've been fighting since Zoe rushed into the restaurant come fully to life.

Finally.

I lean to the side and quietly place my phone on the table. I hold my breath as I unzip my trousers, shoving my hand inside. I bite back a groan as I clutch my cock in my palm. What I wouldn't give to drop my trousers to my feet and shove my underwear down my legs. The damage I could do if I could freely enjoy the rough, bruised skin of my own hand gliding along my length while I listen to Zoe's moans become much less polite and just a little bit louder.

"Oh God," she moans and then sighs contentedly.

I don't come, but the precome is flooding the tip of my dick in a stream.

But I'm close. With a few more strokes and her moans, I could empty my balls on the floor. Or, better yet, I could fall to the ground and crawl to her room and kneel by Zoe's bed. I could let her listen to me while I pleasure myself and wait for her to tell me when to come. I could give her control and let her decide when I got to feel the full power of this release.

I could. I want to. But I don't.

I've never been more disappointed to find that I'm a better man than I ever wanted to be.

I WAKE up to birds chirping, a boat blowing its horns, and maybe even the sound of a stream running calmly down the mountain somewhere in the distance. The world feels bright, good, and full of possibility. I feel like I'm on a picturesque rural vacation.

The signs that I'm not actually on vacation are all around me, though. As soon as I move, my aching thighs protest, and then my back joins the chorus, reminding me of all those steps Alfonso forced me to climb. And though I feel clean, that lukewarm shower did not relax me. And even though I slept very well after a good orgasm, I'm rested but still stressed. If this were a vacation, I would have to reconsider the destination or extend my stay.

I crawl out of bed, and the soles of my feet make every step down the hall and into the kitchen less than fun. I open the refrigerator and grab a bottle of water. I pour a glass and sip it slowly while I look out of the window over the sink and wonder just how the fuck I ended up here. The view has no answers, but I do see a herb garden, a dirt path that leads somewhere further back onto the property, and the top of Nicola's house on the landing below. The scenery is pretty, quaint, but not the vacation destination I would have paid for. Mostly because of all the goddamn steps.

"Buongiorno."

I turn around to see Alfonso padding into the living room in a pair of lightweight shorts, and that's it. There's a thick dusting of sandy brown, almost blond silky hair up and down his arms and legs and across his wide chest and thick, round, protruding stomach.

This motherfucker is testing me, I think immediately. He's gotta be. GOT. TO. BE. 'Cause there ain't no way in hell he's walking out here looking this fuckable for no reason.

"No," I say sharply.

He shoves his hand through his messy hair and then scratches at the nice little bit of day-old scruff growing along his jaw.

"No."

He bunches his eyebrows at me. "No?"

I wave my hand in his general direction. "Just because my sister and cousin let your friends get all in their guts doesn't mean that's what's about to happen here."

He squints at me for a few tense moments before letting out a bark of laughter. "Maybe we should have breakfast before we have any serious conversations. I'm not good at them, anyway."

"No conversation necessary. The answer is no."

He ignores me and continues his path to the refrigerator. "We can make toast from the leftover bread. My brother sent some jam as well. My favorite aunt makes it for the family." He gestures toward the counter, where the last of the fresh loaf is sitting. I grab it and a knife and take it to the table. He meets me there with a small jar of jam.

"Fig," he says. "Can you make some coffee?"

He nods at the counter again, and I see a surprisingly new gleaming kettle and pour-over pot. I'm pretty sure it's the newest thing in the house. I turn to Alfonso with questioning eyes, and he nods.

"My younger brother can't have sex, doesn't drink more than sacramental wine, but he loves his coffee. Everything you need is on that shelf."

I busy myself grinding beans and trying to remember whatever the fuck comes after that because I don't cook, I happily pay someone to clean for me, and people with fancy coffee personality types annoy the shit out of me. I believe in stopping by whatever coffee shop is on my way to wherever I'm going and being content. Kevin was deep in a bougie coffee phase when we met, though, so I can stumble my way through the process, but once the kettle is on, I vow to never do that again.

When I turn back to the table, Alfonso has managed to toast the last of the bread and dig up a bowl of pasta salad that he must have hidden from me last night, and even some cold meat.

"This isn't a bad spread," I say, placing the carafe of coffee in the middle of the table. It might be my only contribution, but I don't believe in comparison for comparison's sake.

He smiles at me. "Well, if I'm going to convince you to... how'd you say it? Let me get in your guts," he bunches his eyes and winks at me, "the least I can do is butter you up."

I open my mouth, uncharacteristically speechless. Zahra would love this. But before I can say anything, Alfonso cuts me off.

"We need butter." He turns back to the refrigerator.

Alfonso

Am I proud that I use up most of the hot water fucking my hand in the shower after breakfast?

I don't believe in shame, so yes, but it certainly wasn't in the plan when I woke up this morning, especially not after last night. Okay, maybe it wasn't completely out of the realm of possibility, but I swear I woke up this morning intent on doing better.

But the way she was looking at me, with wide but still drowsy eyes, and her hand bunched in the hem of her shirt, unconsciously exposing the smallest stripe of her stomach, her ankles crossed as if her pussy needed the pressure...

I'm no saint, and I never claimed to be, but I would never *want* to be for moments exactly like this. I rub my shaft red and raw, using some body wash that smells like the sea. I assume it's my brother's, but it makes me imagine Zoe climbing out of the water, her body encased in something tight, stretchy, and soaking wet.

I spill all over my hand. I watch it collect on the shower floor and then rinse down the drain.

Zoe

I'm still sore.

I wish I could soak in a tub or that I'd had the where-withal to pack some Bengay or a massage bar or something. Anything. Because after another lukewarm — almost cold — shower, I'm beginning to worry that I'll feel like this forever. I hurt so much that I groan when I lower my body onto the couch.

"Sore?" Alfonso asks, walking back into the living room, the smell of a sweet-salty body wash following him.

His question is nice, but the smile on his face is filthy.

I love filth. I appreciate a man who can make damn near every sentence a dirty suggestion, especially if he knows how to follow through. Or if he can be taught.

I wonder which one Alfonso is, and then I glare at him because I'm not supposed to be thinking about any of that.

"No," I spit out.

He laughs.

Someone knocks at the door, and we both turn toward it.

"Get behind me," he says in a hard voice.

Even though it grates my entire soul, I do as he says. I don't want to die. I can stand my feminist ground later.

I move deep into the living room, as far away from the windows as I can get. Alfonso eases toward the door. He mutters a frustrated curse under his breath because he can't see who's on the other side.

The person knocks again and then yells in Italian.

Alfonso's shoulders sag, and he smiles, reaching for the doorknob. He barely gets it open before another man rushes inside and wraps him in a hug.

Obviously, this is one of Alfonso's other brothers. I'd thought Nicola looked a lot like him, but this man could be his twin; he's bigger and more broad-shouldered, his skin is a tanned brown as if he spends his time in the sun without sunscreen, a round belly — a bit smaller than Alfonso's — but long, thick legs, and a surprisingly juicy ass. Must be all the steps. Not that I'm looking. They hug and kiss each other's cheeks and speak rapidly over one another's words. It reminds me of Zahra, Shae, and I under normal circumstances. I reach into my back pocket and pull up the group chat between the three of us, the one Zahra had been avoiding for weeks — since before the wedding.

Actually, Shae had been avoiding it as well, maybe since she got back from Italy. And since I've seen her with Salvatore, I can understand why.

And I hadn't been *avoiding* it per se, but when Zahra and I fell out because I knew she could do better than Ryan's bitch ass and I was the only one with the guts to tell her, I wasn't in the mood to kiki in our sister group chat and pretend like everything was normal. And I guess when I was proven right, and my little sister's life fell apart, she didn't really want to kiki with me either.

I wonder how long we might have gone without speaking if the Council hadn't sent me here.

"Let me introduce you," Alfonso says.

I shove my phone back into my pocket and smile at them as best I can; like I haven't, maybe, just ripped a band-aid off a wound that hasn't yet scabbed over.

"Zoe, this is my brother, Ugo. He's younger than me."

Ugo pushes his brother's shoulder, but he's holding his waist, so it's all for show. I find that incredibly endearing and decide that, of all his brothers, I think I'll like Ugo the best.

I walk toward them, and Ugo lets go of Alfonso to offer me his hand. "Only nine months," he says. "We're basically twins."

"That's what I was thinking," I exclaim as our hands meet.

Ugo might look like Alfonso, but I quickly learn that their personalities are very different. He's warm and a bit awkward, only managing to make eye contact every now and then. And he doesn't flirt with me. I feel more comfortable with him by the moment.

"Who told you I was here?" Alfonso asks.

Ugo's face falls. "Matilde," he says apologetically.

Alfonso rolls his eyes. "So, mamma knows?"

He nods. "I didn't tell her when I found out. I figured you would let us know on your own time. But Matilde must have told mamma. As soon as she woke up, she sent me here to come fetch you."

Alfonso sighs and then looks at me. "Mi dispiace," he says.

"He's sorry," Ugo translates, "but this would have happened no matter what."

"What would have happened?" I ask. I *hate* not knowing what the fuck is going on.

"I'll carry you part of the way," he says.

"No," I say again, with much more force and conviction than this morning when I'd told him that I wouldn't be fucking him. I'd rather fuck him than do what he's about to suggest.

"We can take all the time you need," Ugo says.

"No," I whine. "I fucking hate it here."

We leave almost as soon as Ugo arrives. Zoe tries to walk down the stairs, but I remind her that for every step she takes down the hill, she'll have to walk up one more. She freezes. It's already a warm summer day, but I can feel the heat of her anger as she clenches her fists and then turns around and heads up the steps, glaring at me as she passes.

Ugo laughs, and I push him like I used to when we were children.

We let Zoe set the pace. Besides the fact that she seems like the kind of woman who prefers to be in charge, the steps aren't any fucking easier on me or Ugo, and Zoe's slow, steady climb is just fine for me.

Also, I like the view.

"You shouldn't look at her like that in front of mamma," Ugo says in Italian, dropping his voice just in case Zoe can hear and understand Italian.

Besides the fact that he's interrupted my very important study of the muscles in Zoe's ass — specifically her right cheek — I'm angry at his assertion.

"I can look at my fiancée this way."

Ugo snorts. "Nicola might have believed you. Dario might even try. But we know one another better than that."

I glance at him and then at the sea beyond. I'm not ashamed, but I don't like having to keep a secret from anyone in my family, but especially not with Ugo since he is even more allergic to lying than I am.

"I'm not going to ask why you are here or who she really is. But if you look at her that way, mamma will expect her to stay. Every time you come home, she'll wonder about her, and that'll just be one more thing standing between you two. I know you don't want that."

I look up at Zoe only so that I won't accidentally make eye contact with my brother. She's still just as sexy, but Ugo's words have robbed me of the pleasure of watching her move. Well, some of the pleasure, at least.

"I don't want that," I admit because sometimes I worry that my family thinks I enjoy hurting my mother. I do not.

"I didn't think so," Ugo says casually.

I feel the need to respond. There are a number of things that I probably should confess, but the words that might actually lower my mother's expectations or make her think better of me would ruin my cover, and I cannot. Besides, what Ugo was seeing in my gaze wasn't love, just lust, and I shouldn't be looking at her that way anyway. There's also no use explaining any of this to Ugo because Dario might be a priest, but Ugo's life is just as secluded and celibate.

Salvo sent me here for a reason, to hide Zoe, and that's it. There's no safer place than home, and if anything should happen to me, I can count on my brothers to take care of Zoe and alert Giulio and Salvo. So, I need to focus on doing my job and making sure that the Positano part of my life never meets the Napolitano.

Ugo claps his hand on my shoulder and then jogs the few steps up to Zoe.

He touches her elbow lightly and then points toward the next landing before jogging ahead of us both. She glares at me over her shoulder.

That lightens my mood.

It takes Zoe and I at least five minutes to make it to the landing where Ugo has disappeared.

"Oh my God, my ass hurts. How is that possible?" she groans.

My eyes immediately go to the matter at hand, and I smile.

"Stop staring at my ass."

"Come," Ugo calls. "Have some water."

I gesture for Zoe to follow him through a stone arch that I've likely walked through more times than I can remember.

"You just want to stare at my ass," she mutters.

"Certo. It is a nice ass."

She scoffs. "It better be more than nice when I leave here. All these goddamn steps."

I can't help but smile after her, and not just because my appreciation for the view has returned in full force.

———

Zoe

Alfonso's brother Ugo leads me off of the main steps through a stone archway and into a small alcove. It's not midday, but already the sun is beating down on us. The steps only make the heat that much worse, and I feel like I'm melting. In fact, based on the amount of sweat pouring from my body, I *am* melting. Maybe I won't have to finish climbing up all these steps because soon enough, I'll just drip away and evaporate.

Ugo leads me to a stone fountain that looks like a carved sun with a face and a waterspout as the mouth.

Alfonso comes around me, a reusable water bottle in his hand, and he fills it. I watch him and note the patch of wetness on his t-shirt from his backpack. Not that I'm looking too hard or anything, but the wet cotton sticks to his back muscles, and that's sexy to me, okay?

When Alfonso turns to hand me the bottle, our fingers brush as I take it from his hand, and he watches me as I drink, standing so goddamn close that I swear I wipe the sweat from my chest and some of it lands on his arm. It must be the sun and the jet lag because all of a sudden, I am horny as fuck, but we still have more than fifty steps left to go, and I'm sure that all this excess lust must be sapping my energy.

I'm going to kill Zahra when this is all over; you know, assuming one or all of us don't die in the middle of this mafia war. There's a running list in my head of all her offenses for my eventual defense.

Top of the list is that, because of her Italian disappearing act, somehow I'm on the Council of Aunties' radar again. After some very wild teenage years and fun early twenties that caused my mother to ask her congregation for their continued and abundant prayers, I've been setting myself up to move into my thirties like a lady who's learned to be freaky in private. In all fairness, I also have a list for Shae, but she's pregnant, so I'll wait until she pushes her kid's probably big head out into the world before I consider another homicide, but I will certainly be adding to the list of her offenses until all this is over.

I'm not sure which one of them I should blame for Alfonso.

To be honest, he's not the problem entirely. Now that my aching thighs have really kicked up the pain a notch, I realize that Alfonso — and my intermittent and inconvenient attraction to him — keeps reminding me that I ended up with him by default. Because Zahra didn't want to be separated from Giulio, and Shae is carrying Salvatore's baby. How in the hell did all that happen? And why hadn't either of them told me?

I start pacing, I'm so angry.

"Dai," Ugo says. "If you're going to walk, let's continue. Yes?"

That stops me in my tracks. "How many more steps exactly?"

He looks at me sympathetically. "Do you really want to know?"

Are these stairs how I die? Maybe.

Will my ghost haunt the ever-loving fuck out of my sister and cousin? Absolutely.

"Congratulazioni," Ugo says.

"Please shut up," I wheeze.

He laughs and says something to Alfonso, who clearly curses him in return.

Alfonso touches my wet back, and I shrug away from his hand. "Don't touch me. I feel gross," I whine. "This is the worst day of my life."

"Si," he says, "and I'm sorry about that. Come. We'll go inside, and you can freshen up before you meet my mother."

I whine some more.

"I promise," he whispers softly.

I'm hot, and there's sweat running into my eyes, but I blink at him, confused by the intensity of his words. Maybe it's an Italian thing. Maybe he made that promise in a perfectly normal tone, but jet lag, exhaustion, and a faint memory of him standing next to my bed last night make it very hard for me to be sure. So I nod and follow him through another archway.

This property is a lot like Nicola's garden but lush. At Nicola's — two hundred and fifteen steps away — the garden seemed more ornamental than this one, full of flowers. But this garden assails me immediately with the scent of thyme. Everywhere I look, there's some new row of vegetables or fruit tree. There's squash hanging from the trellis above me and oregano in a long planter to my right. There are braided knots of onions hanging from hooks on the side of the trellis closer to the house and buckets of potatoes sitting in the shade.

"This is Ugo's farm," Alfonso tells me.

"It's beautiful."

"Shhh," he hisses. "Don't compliment him, he—"

"I heard her already," Ugo calls. "Do you want a tour?"

"She wants a shower," Alfonso answers for me.

I glare at him. I don't like when people speak for me, not even when they're right.

When we make eye contact, he apologizes. "Unless you want to spend the next hour in the sun listening to him talking about soil."

I cringe.

"You can thank me later."

"An hour?"

"If you faint from heatstroke. If not," he shrugs, "he can go all night."

"Well, hey, now..." I start to say with a smile on my face.

Alfonso rolls his eyes and turns away, trying to hide his grin, but I see it.

I don't know why I find that so endearing, except that it reminds me of Kevin in its innocence. Something like grief hits me right in the chest. Alfonso sees my face fall, and he squints at me — I feel as if he's done that a lot in barely a day. He doesn't say anything, thankfully, but he looks as if he wants to.

Someone yells from the house, ripping whatever this moment was into shreds.

I turn to see Ugo heading toward a door, but Alfonso grabs me at the elbow and pulls me around the house. "There's a small house we use for unexpected visitors. Ugo uses it most nights. You can freshen up there."

He walks me into a building that could be called a shack by someone who loved it. I do not. "Wait," I say.

I hear a commotion behind me and turn.

Alfonso takes advantage of my distracted attention to drag me into the shack. Thankfully, it's much less terrifying on the inside. In fact, for some enterprising mountain man

— and by that, I mean a white man who always has home-made jerky and fruit leather in their backpack, probably — this would be a dream home. It's little more than a micro-studio, though.

On one side of the room is a full-size bed built into the wall; a rectangle of wood juts out as a bedside table. Next to the table is a kitchenette that takes up the compact corner nearest the door. Actually, describing it as a kitchenette might be too generous. There's one burner set into the counter, an electric kettle, and a small French press. Above this setup are two open shelves with two plates, bowls, mugs, and wine glasses on one, while the other is bare. Directly diagonal to the kitchen is what looks like a bath-room or wet room. It would have to be; it's so small.

There's a square of space in the center of the room, kept neat and clean, and Alfonso and I occupy it all. This is a room meant for one person, and it should feel crowded with the two of us crammed in here. Hell, I should feel crowded with Alfonso looming over me.

But I don't.

"Oh," I breathe, looking around again, pretending as if Alfonso's closeness hasn't made the sweat pouring from my body intensify.

"Ugo renovated it a few years ago," he tells me. I wasn't thinking about that, but okay.

"Is there anything he can't do?"

A proud smile graces his lips. "No." He drops his back-pack onto the bench near the door. "Your clothes," he said.

I'd wondered why he'd told me to bring another outfit but had just assumed that we might be spending the night, which in hindsight was naïve. But in my defense, I have never in my fucking life had a reason to climb over two hundred steps in a single day before.

And I never want to have a reason to do that again.

"I brought some toiletries," he says. "Take your time."

He doesn't mean it that way, but dear Lord, the things my body does when he says those three words shouldn't be allowed, especially not less than a week after a breakup.

We make eye contact. He recognizes my reaction and smiles. But he doesn't capitalize on this moment, much to my relief — or maybe disappointment. Instead, he brushes past me out the door and leaves me alone in this small room that, without him, somehow feels just a little too big.

Alfonso

Things that shouldn't be allowed: Zoe, flushed face, dewy, beautiful, temptation in one thick form.

Things that this already confused trip doesn't need: my dick, heavy and hard in my pants every time I make the mistake of getting too close to her.

Things that push my fraying nerves near the breaking point: my mother, rounding the side of the house and rushing toward me.

Well, at least the problem in my trousers is fixed.

WHAT I APPRECIATE MOST about my mother is that she has a script, and she sticks to it.

Why don't I come home more often?

Have I been eating enough?

When am I going to shave?

Is that a new scar?

Is *that* a new scar?

I normally find comfort in the familiar questions, and I nod and answer when I can, as best I can, usually with a mouth full of food she's been piling onto my plate. And then:

Don't talk with food in your mouth. Who raised you?

This is how my mother shows her love, and I reciprocate by enduring it. The food also helps.

But right now, I wish that she would go back to that line of interrogation because this new one is brutal. I hadn't realized she'd been going easy on me all these years.

"Who is she?"

"Do we know her family?"

"Where is she from?"

"America!? Is this for the citizenship or healthcare? I've heard horrible stories about that place."

"Is she pregnant?"

This question, at least, is familiar. My mother asks if Zoe is pregnant with a hungry gleam in her eye. When we were younger, she used to ask this question every time Nicola and I got caught sneaking out, or she heard we had a girlfriend from some busybody in town, or we even looked at a girl on the street. But over the years, her tune has changed. Dario told me that she often laments how unlucky her life is; four sons and none of them married or even reckless. She asks the priests to pray for our love lives. She lights candles for her future grandchildren. She prays constantly for babies to spoil. Once she starts on this line of questioning, she can't let go. If we allow it, she will talk about all the days we're wasting of her old age by not giving her babies to raise.

"You should get her pregnant. It will be good for your immigration file."

I look desperately over her shoulder at my father and Ugo; they're pretending not to hear her and bending over a bed of rosemary. Traitors.

"Mamma," I say, and she stops speaking, probably out of shock. I normally don't interrupt her. "I've missed you." I grab her shoulders gently and kiss her on her cheeks. She pulls me into a hug, and I hold her. I don't have a plan beyond this. Planning is not my strength. Thankfully, my stomach growls, and she pushes me away.

There's a horrified look on her face.

"Did you eat? Ugo," she yells, "why didn't you let him

eat before he walked up all those steps? And where is Nicola?"

She turns away to fuss at my brother and pick some vegetables from the garden.

I back toward the door, preparing to stand sentry there until Zoe is done. I really don't know what else to do. I wish this was something I could ask Giulio's help with, but he would only laugh if I tried. And of all the things I should call about in this moment, my overbearing mother isn't on the list.

After what feels like an hour in the hot sun, the shed door cracks open. I turn my head enough to peek through the slit without alerting my mother to the fact that Zoe is there. It's still hot outside, but I can feel the steam from her shower. Or her body. I can see her brown eye and a sliver of her bare shoulder. I look away.

"So, that was your mother," she says.

"Si."

"What's our story?" she asks. "How did we meet?"

I'm speechless.

"You *do* have a cover story for us, right?"

I turn toward the door fully and frown. I could lie to her and tell her that I forgot. I could make something up right now and pretend I'd been giving it some serious thought all night. But again, lying is not one of my strengths. "I was worried about getting you here safely; that's it. I haven't had time to think beyond that. I'm terrible at making plans. And lying. I'm especially bad at lying to my family."

She sighs, and then her face disappears from the crack in the door. I'd assumed — hoped — that she was naked because...why not? But when she moves, I can see the striped dress she's wearing off the shoulder, and I frown, but I keep looking.

She sighs again. "Fine," Zoe says and then pulls the door open. I blink up at her. The dress is loose around her body and falls to her feet, but if you look hard enough — and I do — you can see the edges of the curves I felt last night.

She glares at me with serious intent, her lush mouth in a set line and her hands on her ample hips. "Then just follow my lead."

She stomps out of the shed and moves to stand next to me.

I turn in a circle to keep her in my sight at all times, for obvious reasons and some not so obvious. "Certo," I say absentmindedly. In that moment, I think I would do anything she wanted, follow her anywhere.

I jump at her unexpected touch. I look down to see her holding my hand, our palms pressed tight and fingers laced together.

"We have to convince her," Zoe says, her eyes searching mine for understanding. "If your mother's anything like mine, she's been waiting for this, and if we convince her, then everyone else will believe this sham is real."

I nod silently at her, but I don't speak.

I really don't like to lie, but I'm not so in love with the truth, either, especially not when telling Zoe the truth would mean her taking her hand from my grasp.

If this plan fails, at least I'll know what it feels like to stand shoulder to shoulder with Zoe, her warm skin touching mine.

Zoe

On a scale of one to Dedicated Therapy Fund, Alfonso's mother seems like a solid Dodge Her Calls on Weekdays kind of mom, and I respect that energy. My mother is *very* similar, although she fluctuates between that and Aggressive Social Media Helicopter Mom, but that's mostly because I travel a lot for work.

The point is that I'm used to this kind of overbearing but ultimately caring maternal energy, and even though I can't understand a word she's saying, I know to nod and accept every plate of food she offers me.

In fact, not understanding actually makes it easier.

She speaks to me in slow, simple Italian hoping that she will stumble on the right combination of cadence and simplicity for me to understand her more complex thoughts, hoping to bridge the space between her limited English and my nonexistent Italian. She won't, so I hurt my cheek muscles smiling and chewing her food appreciatively.

Alfonso translates for her, but we've devised a system.

Alfonso's mother asks me a question. Alfonso pops a bit of bread or a piece of fruit into his mouth so he cannot translate quickly, slowing down the pace of her interrogation — and then he translates into English what she's asked. But underneath the table, his hand rests on my thigh. If he wants me to answer honestly, he pats my leg. If he wants me to lie, he squeezes lightly.

We pass a surprisingly lovely morning in his mother's kitchen that way. Maria's food is even better fresh, and she practically beams when I nudge Alfonso to tell her how much I enjoyed the leftovers we took from Nicola last night. When she hears that, she yells into the garden for Ugo to bring her some cedro citron and begins to make yet another dish for lunch. I don't know how many people are coming for the meal, but we definitely won't be spoiled for choice.

If I'd met her under any other circumstances, I would have begged to be set up with one of her sons. I even enjoy Alfonso's hand on my leg, but that's neither here nor there. I start to think that if this is what it'll be like to be stashed away in a gorgeous Italian beach town, I might give Alfonso some slack. Besides the stairs, I think I can survive this place.

But then Alfonso's youngest brother Dario arrives, and everything kind of goes off the rails.

I GREW UP BAPTIST.

I'm technically an atheist, but damn near no one knows because my mother routinely lies about that. She doesn't want to admit this failure, as she sees it, and I don't care enough to correct her. Besides, she likes to get the congregation to pray for me, and atheist or not, I appreciate all prayers, good wishes, and pats on the back.

I think all of this because as soon as Dario walks into their parents' house, Alfonso is overtaken by a strong cloud of what I assume is Catholic guilt. I can't actually say that I'm super surprised since his big bruiser façade has been fraying since we arrived at Nicola's house last night. And between Ugo's familiar ribbing and his mother's incessant questions, I've begun to see him as something besides the man who'd nearly beaten a man to death in the street. He was still that, of course, I don't think I'll ever forget it, but he's something else as well.

Or so many other things.

He's a brother, and, depending on which of his brothers

he's interacting with, his birth order comes out in small, endearing ways. He's radiating with proud older brother energy whenever Ugo's around, but he descends into annoyed younger brother status at Nicola's teasing. Once again, they force me to think about Zahra and Shae and all those complicated feelings about their current predicaments that I don't know how to process. He's also his parents' child, and his relationships with them are unique. Maria is overbearing and indulgent, showing her love in attention and food. And while I haven't spent much time in his father Gabriele's presence, I've been watching him out in the garden with Ugo as the two men check on their crops. Unlike his wife, the older man seems to barely speak; he listens intently to his son, nodding every now and again. When Ugo bends down to dig into the soil with his fingers, the older man pats him gently on the shoulder. It's sweet, and I can see how he and his wife have probably gotten along so well all these years.

But the entire mood of the house changes when Dario arrives.

I know every parent says they don't have favorites, but Dario is clearly their mother's. I can tell by the smile on her face and the way she exclaims, opening her arms to him. And my suspicions are confirmed when Ugo and Alfonso make eye contact and roll their eyes behind their mother's back.

Yeah, they're like Zahra, Shae, and me, and that small look makes me miss them.

"It's nice to meet you," Dario says to me.

I haven't been paying attention to the conversation because it was all in Italian, anyway, so the English is jarring. So is Dario's accent. Unlike his brothers, his English has an almost British lilt to it.

I look around, and everyone is looking at me. Except Alfonso; he's glaring at his brother. "Nice to meet you," I say and let Dario take my hand.

For a second, I think he's going to do something creepy like kiss it. I told Zahra when she was seventeen to never trust a weirdo who kisses a strange woman's hand. He doesn't know where it's been, which means he doesn't give a shit where he puts his mouth.

Top twenty tidbits of life advice if you ask me.

Thankfully, Dario doesn't kiss my hand. He shakes it with a kind smile. "We'd begun to think Alfonso would never bring someone home for us to meet. But here he is, and here you are, and engaged, no less."

He knows we're lying.

***

Alfonso

When we were children, my brothers and I used to say that we had to get past mamma and her little spy. It wasn't Dario's fault that he was the baby, and we were so much older than him. But it was his choice to always run to her and tell on us. He grew out of it eventually, but then he became a priest, and instead of mamma's spy, now he's God's.

It is an incredibly frustrating way to think of the little brother who used to follow me around like a shadow. Dario doesn't help the matter by being an observant and kind person who is also easy to talk to. I avoid him as much as I can because I know it would be far too easy to spill the secrets I need to keep to him, and by extension, God and mamma.

The last thing I want is for him to talk to Zoe and put her at ease. Ugo has already seen through our ruse, but at least he can keep a secret. Dario is not nearly so trustworthy, especially not outside of the confessional.

It's terrible to be surrounded by so many people I *can't* beat or threaten or kill to keep my secrets intact.

"Alright, alright," I say, intruding on his conversation with Zoe and grabbing her hand from his grasp.

"We're only speaking, Alfonso. I just want to get to know my new sister."

He says the word 'sister' like it's a joke. Bai, he figured us out much faster than I thought. Maybe I have been away too long.

"You can get to know her *and* keep your hands to yourself," I say. "Where's your collar?"

Dario's only twenty-five, but he looks at me the way that all those ancient priests used to look at us when we fought in mass. That must be a look they teach in seminary. I don't have time to pull Zoe away, to warn her about my brother's preternatural ability to recognize when someone is telling a lie, so I need to tell her in other ways and hope she'll get the hint.

First is to make him look less normal.

Dario smiles good-naturedly and turns to mamma. He tells her he needs to freshen up and then ducks off to the bathroom. Ugo follows papà back out in the garden, and mamma turns to us — Zoe and I — with a smile on her face, her eyes on my hands holding Zoe's tightly.

"Belissima," she says excitedly and turns toward the kitchen. "Pulisci il tavolo."

I sigh and pull a chair for Zoe to sit. I won't make her work, but I need to keep her close.

Zoe

I spend the next hour in the kitchen with Alfonso and Maria. Dario changes, but before he can come back to investigate me, he's called away to visit one of the neighbors. Apparently, there's an elderly woman who won't be able to make it to mass. Maria sends Dario off to check in on her and take her confession. She sends a fruit tart with him on a thin white plate that looks like an oversized doily.

Ugo brings in small baskets of fruits and vegetables from the garden and takes pitchers of citrus-infused water back with him. Their mother shows me how to make pie dough and pasta, carefully explaining each step to me. She promises that next time, we'll do it together. I nod, knowing there's no way in hell.

Alfonso and I peel peaches, apples, and potatoes. I pretend as if I'll remember her recipes, but I don't have to pretend to be excited to eat them. When Dario returns, he has another doily with half a cake on top in one hand and a basket with bottles of olive oil and wine in the other. And then Nicola arrives out of nowhere with a cooler of fish freshly caught from the sea.

All of a sudden, there's a tart in the oven, and we're preparing to have lunch together at the long table in the middle of the garden.

Maria creates a production line. She passes each colorful and unique plate or bowl into my hands and tells me the name of the dish atop it in that same slow Italian. Alfonso translates for me, and I take it out to the long, rustic wooden table with two benches running along each side and matching chairs at either end. Apparently, Ugo made this set as well.

Dario and Ugo set the table and fetch more bottles of wine from the cellar. Their father can make one dish, a salad of lettuce, tomatoes, onions, and capers with a simple lemon and olive oil dressing using some of the olive oil Dario returned with. Everything is either pulled from their garden or the valley, and he makes it at the table. I catch snippets of the preparation as I bring the dishes outside, fascinated. Ugo catches me up on the steps I miss.

It's a surprisingly calm afternoon. For at least an hour and a half, I don't worry about wherever Shae is and what Zahra is doing in Naples. For an hour, Alfonso and I get so good at working together that when his mother asks me to try saying pesce all'acqua pazza, I do, and we're both pleasantly surprised that I don't mangle *every* word, even though I have to wait for Alfonso to translate the name of the dish. I don't even flinch when he throws his arm around my shoulders and tells me that his mother thinks I'll be fluent in a year.

I won't, but we both beam at her as if there's hope.

I don't want to think about them, but I can't help but remember those few holidays I spent with Kevin's family, where I was his and Tyrone's awkward third wheel. Where Kevin's mother looked at me in confusion — because she'd already come to grips with her son being gay, so who the hell was this woman on his arm — and his uncle tried to play footsie with me under the table — because if I'd fuck his nephew and nephew-in-law, *surely* I wanted to fuck him too.

This lunch, however fake, is nothing like that, and so, I give myself permission to enjoy it for whatever it is, but that good feeling only lasts so long.

***

Alfonso

Lunch goes well. *Very well*.

But I feel Zoe pulling away long before Nicola and Dario begin to clear the table.

She still smiles and tells my mother how lovely everything was and keeps smiling while I translate. She lets my father pour her another small glass of wine, but she sips it without any of the enjoyment from earlier in the day.

"Mamma, I think she's tired."

"Oh," my mother exclaims, looking at Zoe as if she hadn't been staring at her for hours. She nods. "She needs some rest. Don't pester her too much at night."

Ugo chokes on his sip of water, and even my father smiles around his wine glass.

"Mamma—" She waves off the rest of my sentence.

"I'll make you some food to take, okay?" she says and pats Zoe's cheek sweetly.

"What's happening?" Zoe asks. "What'd she say?"

Ugo laughs. "Si. Cosa ha detto? What'd she say?" he asks. Stronzo.

"I told her you were tired, and she's going to give us some food for home."

"Oh," Zoe says, her shoulders slumping forward in relief. "I think I am tired. I think the jet lag is catching up to me."

I nod at her, but Dario speaks before I can.

"When did you arrive, Zoe?"

"Last night," Nicola adds helpfully, stacking more empty plates.

"In Italy, I mean," Dario clarifies.

"Yesterday," I bite out. I reach for Zoe's leg, ready to resume our secret system again, but as soon as I touch her, she shudders and pushes my hand away.

"And how did you meet?" Dario asks.

I want to squeeze her leg and tell her not to answer this. I can't. "A man tried to steal my purse," she says. "Alfonso stopped him. He rescued me."

"And *how* did he stop him?" Dario asks.

My back stiffens, and my hand flexes. I don't need to be looking at Ugo to know that he's sat up straight or that my father has reached for the packet of cigarettes in his pants pocket as a reflex; he hasn't smoked in over a decade. And even though Nicola didn't hear the exchange between Dario and Zoe, he knows something has happened while he was away. He begins to clear the last few plates from the table, his eyes darting around to try and catch the thread of the conversation.

I want to tell Zoe to say nothing. To faint if she feels the need. I want her to do anything but respond to Dario's question and accidentally rip open an old family wound. But she's pushed my arm away, and if it is the jet lag finally catching up to her, it's clouding her ability to read the proverbial room.

"What does it matter?" she says in a small, tired voice.

"I'm sorry?" Dario asks.

She turns toward him at the head of the table. Her eyes are dark flints of steel, and her normally soft mouth is hard. I can see her jaw working and imagine that she's struggling to keep herself together in a way that I recognize viscerally.

"I said, what does it matter how your brother stopped a man from robbing me? He saved me. Isn't that the important part?"

When Dario was a boy, he used to screw up his face when thinking deeply about an issue — what flavor gelato he wanted; blue tie or black; sleep or a few more minutes of television. He was the sweetest child. When he joined the seminary, that look went away. The childlike indecision became a haughty intellectual and religious elitism, a surety that God had ordained his train of thought.

I miss that curious and open version of my younger brother.

"Jesus says," Dario begins, and my brothers and I stiffen for a lecture, a sermon.

"I'm an atheist," Zoe says, cutting him off. Why hadn't I ever thought to do that? "Like I said, your brother saved my life. That's more than I can say about the other people on the street who just stood there and watched me try and keep hold of my purse, which had all my money and my passport inside. Save whatever you're about to say for the next girl."

The table has gone quiet. I'm staring at Zoe in awe. We're *all* staring at her, even Dario.

It's Nicola who breaks the silence. "It seems like she's made for you," he says in Italian. He's laughing so hard there are tears in his eyes. Our father laughs with him before turning to Dario. "Take these plates inside," he says in a soft voice that brooks no pushback, not even from Dario, our mother's favorite son.

I watch this exchange in a daze. But then I lock eyes with Ugo. I so wish I hadn't. I know him well enough to know what he's thinking.

She's dangerous, his eyes say.

Believe me, I know, my eyes say in return.

WE HAVE to walk two hundred and fifteen steps down to Nico-la's house. Once again, I let Zoe set the pace. She's distracted and clearly frustrated and speeds down the first nearly one hundred steps, but after she seems to have burned through whatever is on her mind, she slows to a more manageable speed.

"I hate these steps," she mutters to herself.

I nod sympathetically, not that she's paying any attention to me.

"It's hot as hell," she adds. "I feel like I'm melting."

"We're almost there," I try and console her, "and then you can take a shower and cool off."

She turns to glare at me, and my eyes widen in shock. I don't think she's looked at me once since before we left my parents' house.

"The shower is too small," she says irritably.

"What?"

"The shower in my bathroom is tiny. Have you seen me? Have you seen that shower?"

"No," I say quickly. "I haven't, actually. I always use the other toilet. I'm sorry."

Those words catch her off guard, and she stops, turns, and squints at me. "What?"

"When I come home, I don't use that bathroom. And I don't come home often."

"Is that what all that was about?" she asks, pointing up the steps.

I know what she means, and I shift uncomfortably. "Some of it."

She crosses her arms and waits, her chest heaving as she works to catch her breath. I look at her from head to toe because I *really* don't want to have this conversation with anyone, let alone a stranger. The fact that she's a beautiful stranger somehow makes this harder.

Zoe's covered in a sheen of sweat. Her curly hair is sticking to her skin at her temples, and small tendrils cling to her neck and shoulders. Her medium brown skin is flushed a bright red. And her dress — the one that I had appreciated just a few hours ago for giving a hint of her curves — is hugging to those same curves wantonly. There are no more hints, only gorgeous, thick certainties.

"I'm waiting," she says.

I can't help but smile. "We all have our roles in the family. You probably figured it out already, yes? You're smarter than I am." I lean forward, waiting to see if she'll take the prompt.

She watches me for a while and then rolls her eyes. "Dario's the baby, your mom's favorite. Can do no wrong."

I grunt in annoyance and nod for her to continue.

"Ugo's a lot like your father, I think, quiet, hard-working, loves the land."

I nod.

"I can't quite figure Nicola out, but he seems like the kind of person who swans in at the perfect time and then leaves before anyone can ask where he's been."

"Like today," I say. Even though I'd announced that Zoe and I should leave, as soon as Zoe had put Dario in his place, Nicola kissed everyone goodbye, welcomed Zoe to the family, and then slipped out of the garden on his way to who knows where.

Zoe nods. "He's definitely up to some shit."

I laugh.

"And you."

The laughter dies on my lips.

"I can't figure you out, actually," she says in a quiet voice.

"I don't believe that."

She smiles and turns to continue down the steps. It's easy to follow her lead. The sun is high in the sky now, unlike when we'd ascended. We pass a cluster of tourists, making their way up from the beach, it looks like. Zoe waits until they're well away up the mountain before she speaks again.

"I thought I'd figured you out in Naples. Big, scary brute. The muscle. The threat that Salvatore and Giulio use, so they don't get their hands dirty."

If Giulio was here, I think he'd agree with the spirit of Zoe's assessment but would take serious offense to the idea that he wasn't a threat because he is. He understands that he's just a weapon of another sort in Salvo's arsenal. We both know who we are.

But I think Salvatore would smile, maybe nod, and then compliment her, but he wouldn't confirm or deny her assessment. Working with Salvo had taught me that the deadliest weapons seem deceptively benign. Besides those minor details, however, Zoe is right about me and my brothers.

She shakes her head quickly and glances at me. "But then we got here, and now I'm not so sure." She holds her hand out as if to accentuate this point. "I mean, you're definitely dangerous. I'm just saying that I guess now, I don't think that's all you are."

"You're wrong," I tell her, practically cutting her off. "That's it. That's exactly who I am. When we were young, I was always getting into trouble, always fighting, always embarrassing my parents. Salvo helped me turn all that... chaos into a career. But a weapon is exactly who I am."

We walk for a dozen or so steps in silence. I peek at Zoe out of the corner of my eye. She's not looking at me. Instead, she's either watching her feet as she takes each step carefully, or she's looking out at the sea view.

I hate too much silence. Always have. It's how I always got in trouble when I was younger. I didn't like to lie, and I'm not the best at keeping petty secrets.

"Well..." I say.

She looks at me in confusion. "Huh?"

"Do you have anything to say?"

She shrugs. "Nope. I gave up on trying to make men feel better about themselves in college. Waste of time if you ask me. If you say you're a menace, who am I to tell you

you're not? I don't even know you. Oh, thank God, we're here."

Zoe brushes past me on the small steps and marches toward Nicola's gate. I follow her but at a distance, confusion slowing my steps.

Zoe, however, isn't interested in my distraction. "Hurry up," she calls over her shoulder. "I need some water and to get the hell out of this dress."

My eyes move to her body again. "Oh," I breathe, distracted again but in a different way.

FIFTY STEPS away from Alfonso's parents' house, I realize that I'm going to have to reach out to Tyrone and Kevin eventually. At the height of my anger, I wanted to just disappear from their lives, the ultimate fuck you to them for breaking my heart, but I don't think I can do that. I don't have anything to apologize for. I don't want to get back with them. But they do deserve to hear why, as clearly as I can manage. I'd told them during our last night together, but it's so easy not to hear anything when you're yelling. Unfortunately, this realization doesn't help me figure out how to express what I'm feeling in concise words, and I hate being at a loss for the right thing to say.

I'm trying to compose my thoughts into an email in my brain. That's what I'm thinking about when Alfonso tries to get me to expend some emotional labor on him. I will not. Been there, done that; got my heart broken too many times before. I'm good. Gently breaking up for real with my exes back home is all the energy I have for this season in my life — maybe more than I have. Once I do that, I can figure out how to get my foolish sister and cousin the fuck out of this country, and then I can take a *real* vacation. I deserve it. Soothing Alfonso's negative perceptions of himself isn't in the cards for me, fake fiancée or not.

When he unlocks the outer gate, I rush into the garden. I groan at one more flight of stairs. I walk determinedly — but slowly — up to the other house. I'm so tired and hot and sweaty that I plan to sleep for a week. I even think I'll manage not to be annoyed at the tiny shower stall. But when he lets me into the house, Alfonso's hand settles on the small of my back.

I try and squirm out of his grip. I'm hot and sweaty, and my dress is soaked through, but he holds on tight and leads me away to the other side of the house, where I guess he slept last night.

Alfonso leads me into the bedroom. I'm surprised to find his bed neatly made, but I look away. None of my business. We move through the room and through another doorway to a bathroom, tiled from the floor up to the ceiling. I see a shower head in a corner but no small stall.

"This wet room is bigger than Ugo's. I need lots of space. You can shower in here," he says and then turns from the room.

Should anyone be so happy to take a comfortable shower? Yes, and the next time someone tries to tell me that I'm doing too much with my spa time, I plan to punch them. Full stop. If I've learned nothing else from the past two days, it's that a good shower is self-care. Or something equally worthy of being an inspirational quote in a Live, Laugh, Love kind of daily planner.

I have a second wind now. I rush across the house to my bedroom, passing Alfonso in the kitchen, putting away the piles of food his mother sent back with us. I grab all of my toiletries from the bathroom and dig in my suitcase for my emergency spa pack, which I keep always on hand just for moments like this. Well, not 'just like,' but near enough.

When I rush past the kitchen again, Alfonso is leaning against the counter, eating an apple, waiting for me. There's a smile on his face. He waves, and I'm so happy that I wave back.

I shut the bathroom door and decide to take my time.

I work hard.

Sometimes I fuck hard.

And I take my self-care just as seriously.

I have some aromatherapy bath drops, and I squeeze them directly under the arc of the shower spray. I have a bath melt that I put near the drain in the center of the room. I turn the shower on as hot as the ancient system can manage, and after a few minutes...well, it's not as hot and steamy as my bathroom back home, but just the smell of lavender and vanilla soothes me.

While I'm waiting for the water to warm, I wet my hands under the spray and use the exfoliating facial cleanser to wash away an entire day of sunscreen and sweat. I let it sit on my face and step under the spray and then give the rest of my body the same treatment.

My mother is the kind of woman who can spend a full day taking care of her skin, body, hair, and mind, and she did. Once a month, she kicked my dad, Zahra, and me out of the house to "have fun or something." Once she was alone, she took all her butters and oils and other sundries into the bathroom with a bottle of champagne and her tape player. She listened to her favorite music and made herself the center of her day alone. And when Zahra, Shae, and I were old enough to understand, she made sure to tell us that we deserved at least the same kind of alone time and personal attention.

I know she thinks I never listen to her or take her advice — because I tell her that I don't — but actually, that's a lie, and my buttery soft skin is a testament to that fact. Once I'm clean, I turn off the shower and dig a sheet mask from my beauty essentials pack; this one is great for brightening and firming. I have to root around to find the travel pumice stone I keep in here, and then I go to work on my rough heels.

Usually, before a vacation, I pay a number of people as much money as they want to do these things for me. At the very least, I try to get a new set of braids and a pedicure! The Aunties have really ruined my pre-trip preparation, but that doesn't mean that I'm not always prepared. In the warm, steamy bathroom, I exfoliate the ever-loving fuck out of my body until it feels like mine again.

I moisturize myself from face to foot and then look at my reflection in the foggy mirror. I look like myself and smile for what feels like the first time in months, or at least the first time since before my entire life got turned upside down. I feel so good that I somehow forget where I am and who with.

When I pull open the bathroom door, naked and chubby as the day I was born, I find Alfonso standing next to his bed, a pained look on his face and a very prominent, hard column disrupting the pleat of his pants.

"Well, let's see it then," I tell him.

The pained choking sound he makes when I say that is almost as good as the triumph I feel when he does as I say.

<hr>

Alfonso

I grew up in a house full of men, a thing my mother could complain about endlessly. It's one of the things I remember most about my childhood, the way she'd fling open the doors of the house sometimes, muttering to herself, "La puzza. L'uomo. I ragazzi." No matter how old we got, no matter how much puberty changed our height, our smell, or our voices, her refrain remained the same. She'd wanted all girls, she'd gotten all boys — her disappointment didn't stop her from loving us, but loving us didn't erase her disappointment.

To be honest, I never fully understood what she was trying to say. We were clean — unless we'd spent the day at the beach, dipping in and out of the sea, or helping papà in the garden — but I get it now, finally after all these years.

Zoe's smell permeates the house slowly.

Vanilla and lavender.

One minute I'm putting more of my mother's food into the refrigerator, and the next, I can't keep my eyes from darting to my bedroom door.

She left it ajar.

I start to clean the kitchen only so I can keep an eye on

that sliver of space, wondering if the door was open wider would the smell be stronger, would I be able to hear her in the shower?

These are dangerous and inappropriate thoughts, which is why I rush outside.

If I were up at my parents' home, I could have helped Ugo plant or harvest something, but not down here. There are planters with more fruit, vegetables, and herbs, but he's forbidden any of us from touching them without his supervision. Every day, he becomes more like our father.

Since I can't touch his plants, I decide to walk in a circle around the house, which is an obvious mistake. That scent has me so out of my mind all of a sudden that I can't think in a straight line, but I can walk in one directly toward the bathroom window like a fool.

The scent is stronger here.

I groan and then begin my circuit around the house, slowly under that window, faster until I'm back again. I tell time mostly by the sweat beading down my face and body as I walk under the late afternoon sun. I'm burning up from the inside out.

How long can this shower take?

Once my shirt is soaked through, I decide that enough time has to have passed. She has to be done. I must be only smelling the remnants of her shower. Still, I step cautiously back into the house. I kick my boots off at the door since they're now covered in dirt and dust. I move into the kitchen and stand stock still, listening for sounds of her in any part of the house, but I come up empty.

I decide to take that as a sign that she's gone to her bedroom, and I'm relieved. She seemed on edge earlier, and maybe she needs time by herself. I certainly do. I rush into my bedroom. Zoe's smell is even stronger in here, and I groan as soon as I cross the threshold. I pull my soaked shirt over my head and reach for the button on my trousers.

And then the bathroom door opens.

Groan is not a strong enough word to describe the sound that comes out of my mouth.

Last night, I'd seen her in what I thought was her full glory, and it had sent me into a frenzy. This is different, better, worse. She's standing in the doorframe, stream rising from her glistening body, making a hazy shadowed outline of her round form.

The sight of her completely ruins me.

Last night, I had the strength to wait, to leave her bedroom and touch myself in the dark. This morning I made it to the shower, masturbating over her in that same room alone. I don't have that kind of willpower now.

And thank God I don't need to be that strong.

Zoe sees everything.

I noticed that in Naples. While Shae had been almost entirely focused on Salvo, and Zahra only bothered to tear her attention away from Giulio for short spurts, Zoe took everything in. I know because *I* was busy taking all of *her* in. I watched her give my family the same kind of attention earlier, but now that her hard, inquisitive eyes have finally settled on me, well... She already had my full attention; now, she has something more.

"Well, let's see it then," she says.

It's not a request. I prefer that. Unless the solution is to punch, I'm all out of ideas. I live a dangerous life with very few personal stakes — besides death — but it's as if every bit of pressure I've been able to avoid for the past few years of my life decided to converge on my shoulders yesterday.

But Zoe's command takes that weight off my back, and I've never been happier to follow an order.

———

Zoe

I feel every goosebump erupting across my skin. Every raised hair. Every clench of my sex around nothing.

I watch Alfonso slowly undo his pants and push them down his legs, followed by his underwear.

My mouth goes dry at the sight of him.

I don't have a type. I am an equal opportunity whore. My pussy gets wet for all types of men. But Alfonso is tall and stocky, and I like the way the brown hair contrasts with his lightly tanned skin and moves across his broad chest and down to accentuate the curves of his paunch. It forms a thick bush between his legs at the base of his dick, and then it thins over his thighs into a soft dusting.

But it's the patch of thick, bone-straight hair at his groin that gets most of my attention. I don't know why, but somehow it's the sexiest thing I've ever seen, and I'm suddenly very aware of how arousal is affecting my body. Make that make sense — because I can't.

He's semi-hard and thick. The length is nothing to sneeze at — I certainly don't — but Alfonso is all about the girth. I can't help but imagine him filling me up, stretching me as those big hips move between my thighs.

"Touch yourself," I tell him, my own hands cupping my heavy breasts.

He groans. "Where?"

I freeze and tear my eyes from his dick to look at his face.

Okay, I may not have an official type, but bright, eager eyes full of excitement and lust with a thick, veiny dick would definitely go on the list if there was a gun to my head.

"Your chest," I tell him, rolling my nipples between my fingers. "To start."

He grunts and runs a hand over his pecs. Not everyone likes to have their nipples stimulated, but I do, and so does Alfonso. His hips jut forward, and I smile. "Play with your nipples."

God, I love the way he doesn't hesitate. I barely have that order out of my mouth before his hands are moving, so eager to do as I say. "Does that feel good?"

"Yes," he says.

And I don't know how I know, but I do know that that one-word answer isn't the full story. "Twist them." He does, and his hips move again in an unpracticed circle. Bless his heart. "Pinch them."

Oh.

"Harder."

He's leaking from the tip.

"Can you go har—" I have to shove a hand between my legs. Something about the pressure he exerts on his nipples, the muscles that appear on his thick forearms, the way he bites his bottom lip to distract himself from the pain, the way the moisture pools at the tip of his dick and then falls in one long, viscous thread onto the floor.

"Oh," I breathe again. "Grab your dick."

He wraps a meaty, scarred hand around his shaft, and I push two fingers into my wet pussy.

"I want to see you come," he tells me in a rough voice.

"Ask."

"Voglio vederti l'orgasmo," he says. "Per favore."

We both know that 'per favore' is the only part of that sentence I can understand, but it doesn't matter; this moment is all about trust.

"Sit on the bed."

He does.

When I pull my hand from between my thighs, the cool air hits my wet fingers. I slip them into my mouth. I've always loved the way I taste.

To be honest, I want to rush to him. I'm so fucking horny that all I want to do is come as fast and as hard as I can. Hell, I'm so wet that I don't even need him right now. I have a toy in the other room that will have me shuddering and screaming in five minutes max or writhing on the bed for the next hour, depending on the settings. Alfonso's given me enough material to get me off for the next few days, at least.

At least.

But of all the things my exes could accuse me of being, sexually stingy is not one of them. My mother would love it if I developed that skill, but I don't have it in me. The more, the merrier, and one good orgasm deserves another. So, I step in front of Alfonso as my gaze darts down to his wet, hard dick. It's turned a vivid shade of red in the time it's taken for me to get here.

"Are you holding it too tight?" I ask, concerned.

"Do you want me to loosen my grip?" he asks, which is not an answer to the question I've posed, by the way, but it does make the follicles on my scalp tingle.

I make eye contact with him, and what I see in his eyes is...a lot. His face is reddening with arousal — and pain, I'm guessing — but his eyes are calm, serene even. This is the calmest I've ever seen him.

I lift my left leg and place it on his thigh with a hard slap.

He says something that I interpret as a curse, and it only makes me wetter. "Stroke yourself."

His body sags when he releases his dick, but only long enough to lick his hand and then grab himself again. He strokes his shaft slowly, his eyes on my face.

"Do you want to look at my pussy?"

He laughs, and it sounds like a soft, breathless sigh. "I want to see all of you."

It's my turn to laugh. "I'm not hiding much."

He grunts but otherwise doesn't answer. I assume he's too preoccupied.

I move my right hand over the curve of my stomach, and he hungrily watches as I caress my mound in teasing circles and then my clit and my lips.

"Cazzo," he breathes and strokes himself faster.

We both shudder at the sound of my fingers sinking through the moisture toward my opening.

He licks his lips. I watch that red head swell inside his tight grip. His free hand is settled on his left thigh, which is a waste if you ask me.

"Pinch your nipples again."

He nearly knocks me over, the way his body jerks.

"I'm sorry. I'm sorry," he says, but he doesn't stop fucking his hand.

Okay, I need to add that to my list of shit I like, even though I'm not sure how the hell I'd word this specific thing.

I grab onto his head to stay upright. I don't know if that's a good idea, but I do it, and we both moan out loud. I pull him closer, but he doesn't open his mouth for me; he doesn't even beg. He simply keeps getting himself off below me, and I love that shit.

But I test the bounds of his patience when I start to leak onto his lap. The string of curse words he hisses at me only makes matters worse, but since he doesn't tell me to stop, and I don't tell him to shut up, I just assume we've reached a nonverbal agreement. Besides, I'm already so damn close that who even cares about etiquette anymore?

"Gimme your hand," I moan.

He looks bewildered for a second, bless, so I grab his hand from his chest and place it underneath my pussy. This command is mostly for the theatrics since my aim has always been a bit shit, but good sex deserves a little razzle-dazzle if you ask me.

I wrap my hand around the back of Alfonso's head again, and I start to fuck myself with my fingers with all the energy I've got left. I'm moaning and pressing my hips forward. Alfonso is grunting like a beast and jutting his hips up toward my pussy. I don't always squirt, but when I do, it's worth it for me and anyone lucky enough to be on the receiving end of that wet blessing. I appreciate that Alfonso understands that without any prompting.

He's stroking his shaft, shifting his body so I can leak onto his lap and lubricate his dick. He moves his other hand to try and catch the wild spray of my orgasm, and then he pours the bit of fluid he's collected down his throat before rubbing his wet hand over his chest. As if he's marking himself with my scent.

I'm not normally a multiple orgasm type of woman, but there's a first time for everything, and I lose control of myself with that second release.

My fingers dig into the nape of his neck, and then Alfonso's grunting and groaning, he bends forward, and his face rests on my right breast. I can see his palm strangling the head of his dick.

And then he groans against my breast as his fist pulls thick white globs of come from the head. It spills over his hand and seeps through his fingers, lubricating the palm still gliding over his shaft.

"Fuck," I breathe.

"Si, si."

I run my fingers through his hair before I place both hands on his shoulders. His skin is covered in sweat. We both know my hand is wet with my release. He groans when I touch him. I stand on shaky legs and hold on until I feel strong enough to walk toward the door.

"Thanks for letting me use your shower. Bathroom's all yours."

THERE's no nap like an 'I just exfoliated my entire body and came all over a sexy stranger who doesn't talk too much during sex' kind of nap, in my opinion.

I wake up four hours later and stretch like a cat. I push the covers from my body. I'm still very much naked, and the cool air makes me shiver, but after the midday heat, I'm not complaining. And unlike this morning, I finally feel rested. My back and thighs are less sore. I run my hands over my skin, and everywhere I touch is smooth as silk. My room is pitch-black, and I could probably fall back to sleep, especially with some usb-charged assistance, but my stomach growls.

I crawl out of bed and wince. Okay, the rest of my body feels better, but my feet need a little more time. I turn on the light only long enough to dig a robe I don't even remember packing from the suitcase. Thank goodness I keep a travel to-go bag there for a spontaneous trip.

I open my bedroom door, and the rest of the house is dim and very quiet. I wonder where Alfonso is, but not for long. As soon as I walk into the kitchen, the outside door opens, and Alfonso steps inside the door frame, looking at me.

His face is cast in shadow, but I have never met a man who was so loud in his silence.

"Are you coming inside or not?" I ask, turning toward the refrigerator. The cold hits my nipples through the thin robe. Alfonso clomps into the kitchen. The sound of each of his steps radiates from the soles of my tired feet up my thighs and straight to my pussy.

"Are you hungry?" he asks.

"Starving."

He grunts in reply, and I smile.

He moves around the kitchen and begins to pull plates and glasses down from the open shelves. I grab his mother's leftover dishes at random. We work together to get another leftover meal on the table. Since I don't cook, this is the most homemade food I've eaten in years. If not for all these goddamn steps, part of me would never want to leave.

"Do you want some wine?" Alfonso asks.

I lift an eyebrow at him, and he blushes. Not as red as the tip of his dick, but I'll probably never see anything that shade of angry crimson again. Maybe. We'll see.

"I'm Italian," he says, by way of a thin explanation. Alfonso stands from the table. I watch him walk to a wine rack built into a wall by the door.

"Where were you?" I ask his back.

"I needed to talk to Giulio and then check the perimeter. No one's getting in here without me knowing, but I don't want to be too cocky." His voice trips over that last word. He turns around with a bottle of wine and a bottle opener in his hands.

"How's Zahra?" I ask, ashamed that this is the first time I've asked about my sister since we left Naples. I turn away from him to grab two wine glasses hanging from a rack near the sink. I rinse them off and dry them with the dishtowel. I busy myself doing this slowly and carefully because I don't want to have to look at Alfonso, just in case he notices the shame that I feel washing across my face.

"She is fine. Giulio says she's decided to acquaint herself with Italian cuisine."

I turn around and squint at him. "She's been here for over a month. What has she been eating before now?"

He shrugs. "She and Giulio didn't leave the house much before you arrived."

I roll my eyes. "Predictable. And Shae? Have you heard from her?"

"Not from her, but I have spoken to Salvatore. He says that she's been a bit sick."

I gasp.

"Not sick," he corrects quickly, shaking his head. "Nauseous. The baby."

I swallow and return to the table. He watches me for a few seconds and then pours a glass of red wine, offering it to me.

I take it, and our fingers brush, but I can't enjoy it. That shame I felt earlier has kicked into overdrive. I haven't thought about Shae's baby since Naples, and I feel like shit. I take a deep sip of wine. "B-but she's okay?"

He nods. "She is fine."

"How long do I have to stay here?" I whine.

Alfonso's face falls. "I don't know. Salvatore still thinks it's important that we not be all in the same place. Not until we have some idea what's going on. It might be that the threat is elsewhere, and you're safest here."

"If I'm safe here, then why not bring Zahra and Shae here?"

He looks sympathetically at me. "That's not my decision. And..." He takes a sip of wine, his gaze dropping to the table. He looks like he's trying to think of a nice way to say whatever is on his mind. I don't need niceties.

"Say it."

He lifts his gaze and locks eyes with me. His eyes are molten fire. "They wouldn't come here," he says. "Not if it meant leaving Giulio and Salvo."

I suck my teeth and look away.

"You know that I am right."

I decide to stay quiet rather than lie like a delusional teenager.

"You feel responsible for them."

"I *am* responsible for them."

"They are adults," he says. "And in love."

"In lust," I correct, sneering at him.

But he only smiles. "That, as well. I believe in letting people make their own mistakes."

"I don't," I say before I can stop myself, but as soon as those words pass my lips, I realize that I've lied in just the way I didn't want to. "Actually," I amend, "I *do* believe in that, but..."

Alfonso leans back in his chair. "But?" He takes a sip of wine.

"Look, if it were up to me, I would be back in New York

nursing a broken heart over my breakup. You don't have to smile like that," I tell him, rolling my eyes.

"So, you are single?" he asks. "We can talk about that later. Please, go on."

He leans forward and grabs an olive from the bowl between us, and then takes another sip of wine.

I roll my eyes again. "I didn't want to come here. Not yet, at least. All I wanted to do was get Zahra to let us know she was okay, and that would have been fine, but the Council of Aunties is so damn impatient."

"The what?"

"The Council of Aunties. It's what we call all the elder women in our family who think they can meddle in our lives whenever they want."

"And they sent you and Shae here to retrieve Zahra?"

"Yes."

"I see. My mother is similar," he says. "I come home once a year and let her try and convince me to marry some nice local girl so I can give her a daughter and grand-children."

I bristle at that.

"When I was younger, I tried to convince her that wasn't what I wanted out of life."

"What did you want?"

He takes a sip of wine and smiles. "I didn't know. But I did know that Positano always felt too small for me. I'm a big man. I need space."

It takes all of my willpower not to let my eyes drag down his body to remind myself of all I'd seen just a few hours ago. But I agree; Positano is too small to contain all of that.

"And how did she take that?" I ask before sipping my own wine.

He shrugs. "I moved to Naples."

I nod contemplatively and take another longer sip.

"You should try that," he tells me.

"Moving to Naples?" I laugh.

"If you want. But I meant moving. If your family wants to control your life, you can let them, or you can leave."

I shake my head. "That's easier said than done."

"Believe me, there was nothing easy about leaving. But would leaving be easier than trying to control your sister's life? Or harder?"

That question stops me in my tracks. And of all the things I have enjoyed about Alfonso today, what I appreciate most is that he doesn't belabor the point.

He puts his wine glass down and reaches for my plate. I watch silently as he begins to dish up some of his mother's food for me. I'm distracted, but I do notice that he gives me all of my favorite foods from lunch. I don't know how he noticed that, but clearly, he had.

I wonder what else he noticed.

I HEAR the front door open. Slow, cautious steps through the kitchen. By the time those steps head toward my room, I'm out of bed, brass knuckles on my fingers, waiting.

I could have gotten a gun, but that's too impersonal for me.

The knuckles are for Zoe. If I were here alone, I would have left them off, so I could feel every blow and make it last, but I don't want to wake Zoe up.

The steps slow as they get close. I'm waiting behind the door, arms raised, ready.

I don't expect the knock. "Buffoon," Nicola whispers, the door inching open. "Are you awake?"

I drop my arms with a sigh and wrench the door open.

Nicola jumps back with a yelp and then a laugh.

"Be quiet," I tell him, grabbing his shoulder and leading him outside the way he came.

"Where is your fiancée?" he asks, teasing me.

It's nice outside, and the grass is cool on my feet. The

sky is the kind of clear blue that I sometimes miss while I'm in Naples, even though it's the same sky, really.

"Separate bedrooms already?" Nicola asks, still laughing.

"Why are you here?" I deflect.

"My favorite brother is back home. Why shouldn't I come see him?" he says.

I sigh. "I'm not that stupid. What do you need?"

He looks side to side and then steps closer. "What are you and Zoe doing today?"

"Why?"

"Answer the question."

I shrug, "Nothing. Why?"

"I need to sail back to Capri to pick up...a package."

I curse him. "What have you gotten yourself into?"

"I could ask you the same question. Shall I?"

We stare at one another as we so often did as children. We could be here for hours. "What do you need us to do?"

"I just need you two to come to Capri with me and spend the night."

"Spend the night?"

"I have a friend who owns a hotel. It's beautiful. You'll enjoy yourself, have a little holiday, and then tomorrow morning I'll bring you back. That's it."

"Nicola," I bark, much louder than I planned.

He holds his hands up and backs away. "Before you bite my head off and tell me no, consider that it is much harder to get to Capri than Positano, and you can slow down whoever you're hiding her from." I shake my head. "And if you're in Capri, then mamma cannot come down here and start planning your wedding."

I stare at him while I think this over, but he knows that he has convinced me. The last thing I want is to have to explain to my mother and Dario why Zoe won't be converting to Catholicism.

The front door opens, and I turn around to find Zoe in that same sheer robe from last night. My mouth goes dry, and every muscle in my body hardens.

"Buongiorno, sorella," Nicola calls.

I move in front of him to block his view of her even as I squint, desperate to see her nakedness again. I dreamed about her all last night.

"What's going on?" she asks warily.

"We're going on a little trip."

Zoe

"Now, *this* is what I'm talking about," I say with a smile on my face.

Nicola has a small yacht. I think. I don't know shit about boats, and I don't care. But I am lying on the deck of his boat in a yellow bikini I found in my suitcase, and I am loving life. The sun is warming my skin. The sea is misting over my body. This ride almost makes the more than two hundred steps I just trudged down worth all the effort. I mean, this is some luxury vacation or an early 2000's rap video type of shit, and I see now that this is the life to which I deserve to become accustomed.

I can hear my mother in my head telling me maybe I could find a man who could give me this life if I worked less or was less 'free' — the word she uses because 'kinky' gives her hives — but I drown her out. Well, Nicola drowns her out by honking the boat's horn, and I thank him for that. Because my mother is wrong: I deserve this life on my terms.

Alfonso clears his throat.

I roll my head to the left and pull my sunglasses down the bridge of my nose to look at him.

His sunglasses are still firmly on his face, but I can tell where he's looking. At me.

First of all, how could he not be? This yellow bikini is my favorite for a reason. It covers the best bits, but barely; that's not its job. The job of this bikini is to remind everyone who sees it that the person wearing it is the baddest bitch with the best ass. I know because I've lost time staring at myself in the mirror while wearing this suit. Alfonso is experiencing the power of this bikini under the best circumstances. The sunscreen, seawater, and a hint of sweat have made every inch of my skin shine.

And the other way I know that he's giving me all of his attention is by the lovely hard girth of him down one of the legs of his shorts. I lick my lips, and he groans.

"We'll be arriving soon," he tells me.

"How soon?"

He turns and looks over his shoulder toward the shore.

Not to be pervy, but I take that moment to enjoy the way his t-shirt stretches over his right shoulder and chest. I lick my lips again.

"Fifteen minutes," he says before turning back to me. "Longer if the queue at the pier is backed up."

"Oh," I say, pushing my glasses back onto my face.

"That's plenty of time. Come get me when you're close." I pull my glasses down again and wink at him. "I mean when *we're* closer."

He grunts, and I smile before leaning back onto my seat. I close my eyes and get comfortable again.

But Alfonso doesn't leave.

The yacht's deck has a sunken area with soft, reclining very fancy, cushioned seats. I feel the seat next to me shift when Alfonso sits all too close to me.

"Your brother can see you."

"Is there something he's not supposed to see?"

I push my glasses down and loll my head to the side to look at him. He turns toward me, but he doesn't remove his glasses, so I do it for him, pushing them up onto his head.

"Why are we going to Capri? Did something happen?"

"No. My brother needed our help."

"Doing what?"

He sighs and shakes his head. "I'm not sure."

"Oh," I tease, "I guess you're not the only bad boy in the family." He looks conflicted about that. "So, what do we need to do?"

"Nothing. He wants us to spend the night at a hotel, and then we'll go back to Positano tomorrow."

I turn on my side.

We're closer than I realized, and he shudders when my breasts, stomach, and thighs press against his body. "Merda, Zoe."

"Let me get this straight," I tell him, leaning forward, letting him feel the weight of me on him. "Your brother is out here committing crimes, and to help him, all I have to do is go on a vacation from my kidnapping."

"I haven't kidnapped you," he says, sighing, never taking his eyes from my cleavage.

"Can you be that kind of criminal?"

He leans into me now and lifts his head to meet my gaze. Our mouths are so close, closer than yesterday when he was using my orgasm as lubrication. Close enough to kiss.

"Do you want me to be that kind of criminal?"

I like Alfonso's mouth. The way his lips move. They're not the plumpest set I've ever let please me, but I think he could use them well. Although it's his tongue that excites me the most. The way it curls around his words and peeks between his lips as if it's trying to tempt me into saying hello.

I bend my right knee and lean into him.

"Harder?" I ask.

He grunts and nods his head once.

I lean into my knee, aiming the blunt tip into the base of his dick.

He makes this delicious sigh of a moan. "Più forte. Harder." When I give him what he wants, he closes his eyes and shudders, clamping his mouth shut to muffle another moan. No man has ever made me this wet with just a sound before.

I feel the wet patch of his orgasm along my shin, and I rub my leg up and down hard, smearing that wetness into my skin and his clothes.

He groans loudly, but the sea steals that sound.

"Interesting," I breathe.

Nicola calls down at us from the steering wheel. "Arrivati! Benvenuto a Capri!"

"WHEN YOU GET to the hotel, tell Sara that Nicola sent you."

When we get off the boat, that's all Nicola tells me before darting into the crowd at the port and disappearing. I could strangle him, and if I didn't have Zoe beside me and the sticky feeling of drying come along my right leg, I would have done just that. But he's gone before I can get my bearings straight. My mind is sluggish after Zoe made me come with only her knee pressing into my dick. I don't even know how she did that. But I can't linger here longer trying to figure it out or find my brother again.

I hear someone whistle, and I know instinctively that it's aimed at Zoe. Of course, it is.

She's shimmied into a pair of shorts and a tank top, but somehow, it feels as if she's still nearly naked. I'd been so distracted by her in that damn bikini that I hadn't been able to focus on figuring out what Nicola is actually up to. And now, my brother is gone, and Zoe's body is still driving me out of my mind. But not just me. I scan the pier, and there are men and women staring at her with wide eyes and slack mouths. I cannot blame them.

And Zoe is soaking up the attention.

We packed all of our clothes in one bag, and I throw it over my shoulder. I place a hand in the middle of her back. "Andiamo, solarità."

She smiles at me, and it's almost too much to take. "What's that mean?"

"Let's go," I tell her, hesitating, "sunshine." My eyes dart to her breasts.

"You're very cute," she whispers, leaning into me. I could happily lose myself in the pressure of her soft skin molding against my side. "But if there are more than five steps, I will step on your dick."

I grunt, and my cock makes a feeble attempt to push more come from the tip.

"Good to know," I say in a hoarse voice.

"I was just thinking the same thing."

There's a strong chance that the hotel room Nicola has arranged for us will just be a spare bedroom in a stranger's home. I don't tell Zoe that because I don't want to distress her any more than is necessary. Besides, I have enough money to find us a room somewhere. But I'm as shocked as Zoe when we step from the taxi and find ourselves at a beautiful hotel.

We walk into the lobby.

Buongiorno," the woman at the front desk calls to us. "Welcome to Hotel Vulcano."

"Hi," Zoe says with a wave.

I walk to the counter, look at her nametag, and see that this is Sara. "Nicola sent us," I tell her. It takes a lot of effort not to let my skepticism seep into that sentence.

Sara's smile doesn't falter, but she does look left and right before sitting quickly at the desk.

Zoe and I look at one another, and she raises her eyebrows, asking me what's going on. I don't know.

But as quickly as the mood shifts, Sara stands abruptly from the desk. "I'll show you to your room, si?" She's speaking much too loud not to be deceiving someone.

I sigh and reach for Zoe again.

"Are we going to get arrested?" she whispers. "Because I'm not getting locked up wearing this."

I look at her again. "I'll let you know if I think you should change."

"Great, thanks."

We follow Sara through the lobby into a courtyard overrun with lush bushes and tall trees, circling a fountain inlaid with a beautiful mosaic of tile and volcanic glass.

"Oooh," Zoe breathes as we walk around it. I nod.

Sara leads us through another courtyard, past a pool that makes Zoe smile at me without a hint of seduction, only happiness.

I've thrown my arm around her waist, and I squeeze her into me. We *are* pretending to be engaged.

"Here you are," she says, not as obviously loud as before. She unlocks the door and leads us into a bungalow. Sara shows us quickly around the small but luxurious room. When we're in the bathroom, she leans forward and whispers, "If anyone asks, you're an American singer with her Italian manager having a tryst on Capri where no one knows you."

"Di cosa stai parlanda?" I groan.

"Got it," Zoe says, taking the key from Sara's hand.

Zoe

"Do you want to go on a tour?" Alfonso asks.

"Not really, no."

"We can take a boat to the other side of the island. You should see Anacapri."

"Why?"

He goes quiet, and I let him figure out an answer.

While Alfonso is trying to convince me to put on clothes and shoes and maybe even a little makeup so that we can pretend to be tourists, I'm floating in a warm pool. There's a canopy above us blocking the sun, but I close my eyes and just coast. Like the boat, this is the kind of vacation I needed.

"I don't know, but I think you should see it," he says weakly.

I sigh and sink under the water. Alfonso's sitting on the edge of the pool, and I swim toward his feet. When I pop up next to him, he jumps, even though we both know that he's been hovering on the edge of the pool, watching me like a hawk. I cross my arms and rest the side of my head on them, looking up at him.

Alfonso is staring at the water, trying to see my body clearly through the shimmering blue.

"Is there a reason you want to play the happy tourist?"

He shakes his head. "The island is beautiful. I just thought you'd want to see it."

"That's sweet." I push away from the edge and then slide between his legs. He gulps and straightens his back, but his hands move to his lap to cover the erection tenting his shorts. I've already seen it, though. "Do you think that a famous American singer brought her Italian lover here to go on a sightseeing tour?"

He rolls his eyes and looks away, but only for a moment. I've been told that my cleavage looks great between a man's legs, and Alfonso seems to agree.

"The rumors could be a lie," he said.

"Not if I have anything to do with it."

His eyes lift to my face, and he looks like he's fighting some battle behind his eyes. I would wonder why, but I think I've already figured it out. I move my right hand to his left knee and rub his thigh softly. He curses lightly and grabs the bulge between his legs.

I want to laugh, but I also want to take this seriously, even though I'm not sure why.

Alfonso's face is turning red, and he's sweating, but his gaze is focused on me. We're concentrating on this together.

I cup his knee with my palm and set my nails against his skin. I take a moment, and then I dig my nails in deep.

He sucks in a sharp breath and holds it, but he doesn't blink.

I dig my nails in deeper. And deeper.

I can see his hand working over his erection.

"Exhale," I tell him, and the air rushes out in a great moaning gust. I move the hand he's using to hide his erection out of the way so I can see. He's using his flattened palm to rub the length of his shaft furiously up and down.

I lick my lips and pull the hand I'm holding into the water, and his fingers snake into my bathing suit top. He starts massaging my breast and rolling my nipple between his digits. I release the pressure of my nails.

"Don't," he whispers. "Please."

"You like pain?" I ask him gently.

"I—" He licks his lips and shifts his eyes away.

Well, that won't do. I dig my nails into his skin again.

He moans and brings his gaze back to me, his own fingers scrambling on his other leg to pull his pants leg up.

"Oh, hello there," I say to the bright red mushroom head of his dick now peeking out of the leg of his shorts.

He covers it with his hand and begins to rub it furiously.

I smile up at him. "So... Pain?"

"I like to fight," he says, his eyebrows bunched in concentration. Or confusion?

"Great way to get hurt," I concede. "But have you ever let someone hurt you in bed?" I push my hand up his leg, my nails sliding across his skin with a pressure that he clearly enjoys.

"No," he groans, sagging forward and grabbing both of my breasts under the water. "Not exactly."

Just then, there's a splash behind us. We turn to see a man who's appeared completely out of nowhere — since we weren't paying any attention to anyone but one another. We watch as the man swims the length of the pool. When he gets close, the force of his body disturbs the water and pushes me against Alfonso's hands. He begins to tweak my nipples lightly, much more gently than I'm treating his thigh. I scratch at his legs with growing pressure, but I'm careful not to break the skin.

When I whimper, Alfonso sighs. "Is that what you like?" he asks.

I turn back to him and lick my lips. "Please, be more specific."

"Do you like to be watched?"

"Yes, but that's not it."

He keeps stroking my breasts, and I want to crawl into his lap so he can suck on them. "Tell me."

"The breakup I should be at home getting over?"

He nods.

"My mother hated that relationship because I was dating two men."

His eyebrows lift.

"They'd been together for years before I met them."

His mouth falls open.

"My *thing*," I tell him, lifting a hand to cup his face and pull him closer, "is that one man isn't usually enough for me."

Our lips are touching, and Alfonso's eyes dart to the side, looking for the swimmer or making sure that no one is watching. I'm surprisingly uninterested in anyone else but him. It's enough just to know that Alfonso is aware of the swimmer's presence, and he's still caressing my breasts in the water.

"Harder," he breathes.

I smile against his mouth and then scrape my fingers down his thigh.

He cries out, and I cover his lips with mine, tasting his excitement.

The warm evidence of his release lands in a wet spurt on my chest.

ZOE and I leave the pool as soon as I come. It seems prudent. She also thinks that it adds to our cover that we slink away back to our room when a large group of tourists descends on the pool. She puts on her dark sunglasses and looks away from the crowd with a smile.

I think she's enjoying this just a little too much, but if it makes her happy, I'll go along with the ruse for her sake. I shield her from the crowd, grab her hand, and rush her back to our bungalow. She doubles over in laughter as soon as I unlock the door.

"This is great. I haven't had this much fun in years," she says.

"I'm glad you're enjoying yourself."

"Well, if I'm going to be kidnapped…"

"For the last time, I haven't kidnapped you," I say, which reminds me that I need to check my mobile. I, of course, told Giulio that I was taking Zoe away from Positano. I expected that he would object, but he hadn't responded before we climbed onto Nicola's boat, and the message I see when we get back to the hotel room is unexpected.

"Be careful. Zahra says to show her sister a good time."

I gulp down that message, and my thigh twinges in a delicious reverberation from the scrapes on my leg straight up to my dick. I'd argue that Zoe's been the one showing me a good time, but I don't think this is what Zahra or Giulio had in mind.

"Sit."

I fall into the desk chair before I even understand what she's asking or why.

"Hold this." She hands me a first aid kit and then grabs the other chair across the room. She places it in front of me and then sits. She opens the small box and rummages around until she finds what she's looking for.

"This shouldn't sting," she says, pouring some liquid onto a cotton pad.

"I don't mind that."

She looks at me with a small smile on her face. "Tell me just in case you do."

I nod. It does sting, but I'm used to the sharp pain of alcohol on a wound. This isn't even the worst I've ever felt. This is barely a mosquito bite. But I like the contrast of that sting and the soft way Zoe touches around the deep welts she's left in my skin.

"So, you never realized that the pain got you off?" she asks, her head bent over me.

I take a deep breath and give this some thought; thought I should have given it before. "When I was little, my mother used to tell everyone that I had a death wish or that I was sent here to scare her into an early grave."

Zoe looks up at me with big, worried eyes.

I smile. "She said I didn't understand fear or pain. I believed her until I was a teenager."

"What happened then?"

I shrug. My smile deepens.

"Nicola and I used to go to Naples on the weekends with our friends. One night, we stumbled into a fight club of sorts. It was mostly just delinquent kids with nothing to do, betting a few euros on the winner. But a few euros was more than I had in my pockets at the time, and I was good at it. Some boys got hit once and were done. Some could take anything but face hits. But I could take it all."

"Because you didn't feel it?"

I shake my head. "I felt it all. Every hit. Every scrape. Every split lip. None of it stopped me; it spurred me on. I liked it. Soon enough, I was the best bet no matter who I was facing, and then I got scouted."

Zoe sits up in her chair and grabs the first aid kit from me again. She pulls out a tube of some kind of medicine. "Scouted for what?" She squeezes some of the cream onto her index finger and then bends over my leg again.

"Amateur boxing."

"That makes sense."

"I thought it did, but the gloves and the padding..."

"Oh," she says, nodding as she dabs the cream onto my wounds. "Not enough stimulation. Got it."

The word 'stimulation' makes me squirm in my seat. She grins up at me before getting back to work.

"But then I met Salvo."

"And how'd you do that?"

"He came to one of my fights. Giulio bet against me, the stronzo. But Salvo said he saw something in me he liked. He bet all his money that I would win against one of the best amateur boxers in Rome."

"And you won, I'm guessing."

I laugh, remembering my last amateur fight. "Of course, I did, but that fighter had a bad habit of talking trash during his matches."

"Okay?"

"Apparently, most people just let him do it. But I'm not most people."

Zoe is watching me with interest, a heat in her eyes that I'm not even sure she realizes is there. "What'd he say?"

"He called my mother a whore."

Zoe gasps lightly. "Did you kill him?"

I have spent the last two days trying not to feel anything for her, especially not the lust that has been consuming me, but now I know that I've failed miserably. The lust is one thing, but the way that gasp makes me feel is something that I've never even fathomed before. And seeing an echo of the bloodlust I felt during that fight makes my heart pound against my chest.

I think I see now how Giulio and Salvo have gotten themselves into their individual predicaments. And I don't know what the fuck is going on in these women's genes, but it's kryptonite, apparently.

"They had to pull me off of him. Salvo hired me that night."

"You know, if you ignore all the details, that's actually a really sweet story."

I laugh so hard I cry.

Zoe

I tell Alfonso that my feet still hurt from all those steps and that I don't want to venture too far from the hotel, which is true. But really, it's because I know I'm going to fuck him, and I have no idea what the Italian laws on public nudity look like, so I want to stick close to home if you will.

We have dinner in the hotel restaurant. I don't have anything too fancy, so I wear a dress that's really just a sarong tied around my body. It's skimpy and scandalous, which I think fits our cover story well.

At the very least, it makes Alfonso's face redden and his dick hard. I wear my sunglasses until the sun sets to feed the rumor that I'm famous. Most of the people in the restaurant are with some random Australian tour group that seems desperate to believe that there's a celebrity in their midst. One table sends Alfonso and I a bottle of champagne. Another watches us for so long that their food grows cold. Some man asks for my autograph. I sign it 'Lena Horne.' He doesn't notice because he's too busy staring at my breasts.

The food is good too.

And not to be sentimental or excessively horny, but I think my favorite part of dinner is when it's over.

"Let's walk around the garden," Alfonso offers.

"If you want," I say. "Although we both know what's about to happen."

He gulps loudly. "Then we should walk and give our food some time to digest."

His arm circles my waist again. I realize just how much this man has been touching me in the past two days and that I have enjoyed it more than I would have expected. I look away so he can't see me smile.

The hotel gardens aren't lush, but there are tall trees and beautiful flowers scenting the air. The paths wind in a maze through the trees. I trick my brain into believing that Alfonso and I are on a private island, just the two of us. We follow a winding gravel path through the garden, and the already blue-black evening sky disappears at points under the canopy high in the air.

If Tyrone were here, he would have pulled out his phone, adorably desperate to figure out the name of every plant we passed. And Kevin would have wanted to take dozens of pictures, so we never had to forget this trip. If they'd been here with me, I would have appreciated their enjoyment as much as I always did; I would have hung on the edges of their pleasure, soaking up only what I needed. But it's different with Alfonso because *he's* the sponge.

He doesn't mean to, but I can feel the yearning black hole of him. He's waiting for me to tell him what I want and precise instructions on how to give it to me. There's so much about his neediness that I enjoy — and that unintentionally speaks to the also greedy black hole inside of me, and my pussy as well — but that is so much goddamn responsibility.

I hate the way that this quiet walk helps me realize that maybe, just maybe, my mother was right. Maybe Tyrone and Kevin weren't meant for me. Maybe I had been with them because I hadn't wanted to grow up. Maybe our arrangement, where we didn't talk about the future and avoided the fact that we didn't want the same things out of life, was a reprieve. Maybe that relationship had been a convenient way to forestall building a life of my own.

It would explain an uncomfortable amount about our lives. Why they'd ever thought they could convince me to get pregnant. Why I refused to move in with them, even though I knew they wanted that. Why blending my life with anyone else's has always been expressly off the table.

Alfonso isn't asking for any of that, thank God, but there's an ease with him I hadn't thought was possible. A tension, as well. He holds me against his side as we walk, waiting silently for my directions but not asking for anything I don't want to give.

I don't want to end up like Zahra and Shae — emotionally committed to these random white men — but I have enjoyed so much of my time with Alfonso. I'm not sure how to feel about this, but there's no reason to pretend it's not true. Actually, there's no reason to pretend as if he and I have a future. Whatever the fuck is happening right now is some alternate universe of my life. It doesn't have to mean anything unless I want it to, and I don't.

What I want is to fuck him, and I decide to just focus on that and forget everything else.

Alfonso looks calm, but his eyes keep darting my way. His nervous, adorable attention touches me. It's not Kevin and Tyrone's cute blerdiness, but I won't ever be able to replace them. However, I do have to learn how to let them go.

And as Mina said, the best way to get over a man, or

two, is to get under another one, at least. She always has great life advice.

There are romantic alcoves all around the garden, with small benches tucked neatly inside the foliage. They give a sense of privacy, but even if they didn't, I would be drawn to them because what I like most is the patches of silky darkness under the canopy. The way Alfonso's big hand flexes down to my hip when he thinks we can't be seen, the way he tells me how desperate he is for whatever I'll do next with his body instead of his words.

I don't know how long I want this kind of responsibility, but tonight, I take it on. I deserve it, and he wants to give it to me so badly.

I think the only being on planet Earth who's *really* shocked that I push Alfonso onto one of those benches is a stray cat that darts across the path when we intrude on its little home.

"I'm sorry," I call softly after it.

Alfonso is much less sympathetic. He pulls me onto his lap and palms my ass, settling me right on top of his already growing erection. "It'll be alright," he whispers against my jaw. "Don't let it distract you from your plans."

"You think I had plans?"

"Have," he says. "And yes. I bet you've thought of things I can't even imagine."

I turn my head and run my mouth along his jaw. "I don't know," I say, "you might surprise me."

He shakes his head. "I'm an ass," he says.

"I don't like the way you talk about yourself," I tell him, confused and annoyed.

He sighs and gives me the softest smile. "I work," he clarifies. "Even my mother has to admit that I'm good at that. You tell me what to do and how to do it, and you can consider it done. Unless it's pain," he adds, letting me feel his smile on my skin. "I can manage that on my own."

Not for nothing, but I can't believe how happy he sounds now that he's realized this thing about himself and that I helped him get there.

"So you want me to do all the heavy lifting?" I ask playfully.

And I know he knows that's a metaphor, but I also know that he's realized by now that being picked up by a man who can do it safely might turn me on just a little bit. And then he lifts me, only so he can shove his hand underneath my sarong and sit my pussy down on his open palm.

I cover his mouth with mine because he's been grunting at me for two days, and I want to taste it, so I do. I grind my wet pussy harder onto his hand for good measure.

Alfonso

I have spent a lot of my life feeling as if I didn't belong. Too big. Too tall. Too brutal. Too rough. That's why I prefer to follow orders; they make me feel as if I belong somewhere. Some part of me matters and is useful, even if it's only my fists.

But Zoe's body makes me feel as if I'm useful for something besides hitting and breaking. I can be careful. I know how to be gentle when I want to be, and I want to be all those things and more for Zoe.

She grabs onto my face and kisses me like she's been wanting to do this all through dinner, which is exactly what I wanted. Her tongue strokes mine forcefully. I want to tell her that she can be a little rougher with me, as I have with other women before, but I don't have to; she already knows. I've never relaxed with anyone the way I do at that realization.

I let myself focus on her pleasure. My fingers glide through her soft wet lips and bump against her hard clit. I tease her opening, circling it, tapping it, pushing my finger inside just enough to make her shiver on top of me, and then I retreat.

She smiles and licks deep into my mouth as I begin to tease her again, with two fingers this time.

I touch her until she soaks my fingers, and I can feel her excitement running down my digits and into the palm of my hand, a wet spot forming on my pants. I caress her perfect cunt until her hole is clenching around me, trying to pull me inside. Until she can't stop shivering or moaning into my mouth. Until she pulls away from me and demands, "Fuck me with your fingers already."

"Finally," I groan and then sink those fingers as deep inside her as they will go. It's still not deep enough.

I hold onto Zoe's waist with my right hand, and together, we guide her hips into a tight circle without losing any contact between my hand and her sex. I refuse to not touch her.

Zoe closes her eyes and grinds her clit onto the heel of

my hand. The groan that falls from her mouth is so loud that I'm certain someone will hear. I don't care. She will care, however. Zoe will like it if someone hears us or stumbles upon us, and I want her to wring every bit of excitement from this moment, so I fuck her harder.

Still, "More," she groans, pulling the knot holding her dress together free. She's completely naked in my lap, but she doesn't give me time to appreciate that before pulling my mouth to her chest and pressing her nipple against my lips.

On another woman, this keening moan would have been a plea, but when I hear it from Zoe's mouth, I recognize it as a command that I'm all too happy to obey.

Come ho avuto questa fortuna? Where has she been all of my life? And how do I fuck her hard enough to keep her?

"Oh my God, yes," she moans, now very obviously riding my hand.

Somehow, this is the best thing I've ever felt, but not enough. I want her on my cock. I want all this wet, clenching softness milking me until there's nothing left.

"Condom," she whispers into my ear, her voice a high-pitched but still commanding wail.

I cannot believe how fast my dick shrivels to nothing but a sad husk. I pull back, letting her breast graze my bottom lip. "I-I don't have il preservativo."

Zoe blinks down at me. "Huh?" She's still clenching around me, but my fingers have stilled.

"I don't have a condom," I say in a hoarse voice.

She smiles. "Sir, I am always prepared. I just thought you would have one closer to hand." Her purse was slung over her arm, but in our rutting, it's fallen into the crook of her elbow. It's nothing more than a small leather pouch, and I'd wondered why she even brought it to dinner. Now I know that she had a lipstick, some gum, and a condom inside.

Beautiful and in control.

And her hand is in my pants.

"Cazzo," I yell the minute I feel her fingers in my underwear. It's as if the world has sped up and closed in on us. I lift my hips, and we both shudder as my fingers press into her again.

"God, I need your dick."

If I weren't on the verge of coming in my pants again, I could have cried. Zoe needs me. Well, my dick, but that counts as surely as my fists. "It's yours," I moan as she fishes me out, stroking me. "Harder."

I'm not the only one who knows how to follow directions.

"Your dick is lovely," she says as her thumb circles the head. "Thick. Not too long. Fat."

I pump my hips up at her at that last word. The way her mouth loves it, caresses it, even. As if my thick, not too long, fat dick is in her mouth. "Dio," I moan.

"But I'm not like my cousin," she says.

"Che cosa? Chi?"

She understands my questions well enough. "Shae," she says.

I wonder why the hell we're talking about her, but out of loyalty to Salvo — and fear that Zoe will take her hand away — I try and focus on her words and resist the urge to fuck up into her hand just yet.

"I'm not going to let a stranger fuck me raw and get me pregnant."

"What?" I shout, my head clearing. "I don't want children."

Her hand stops, and she stares at me.

It's too dark in here to see her face clearly, but I can hear in her shuddering breath that she's surprised.

"Right now?" she asks. "You mean you don't want kids right now."

I move her hand from my dick. "I don't ever want to have children. That is my mother's dream for me, not my own. I told you that already."

I don't understand how a once beautiful moment has turned so sad, but it has. I don't want to talk about children or our families. I don't want to talk at all. I want to fuck. I have wanted to fuck Zoe since the first time I saw her. I'm so sad that I begin to put my dick away; it feels strange having it so exposed in a moment like this.

But Zoe's fingers brush my wrist. I look up.

She takes a shallow intake of air. "I don't want kids either. That's why my last relationship ended."

I don't know why she's telling me this, but I can see that she feels better admitting it to me. I don't care about children. I don't care about her last relationship. I care about her pussy, and if she smiles or is tired or sore. I care about her fingers ripping the condom open.

"Mio Dio," I groan. There's not quite enough time for my mood to catch up with my brain or my cock. Zoe's hand is faster, rolling the condom down my shaft, pulling my fingers from her cunt, using her own wetness to lubricate my dick.

But I am fully caught up on events when she grips me at the base and then lines up the head of my dick with that grasping hole. She waits for me. My hands go to her waist, and my fingers dig lightly into her skin. Still, she doesn't move.

"Tell me what you want," she says.

I could come at those words alone, but I won't miss the moment to say the words that have been filling my throat for days. "Fuck me," I yell. I don't care who else hears.

The sound we make when we come together is music. Filthy fucking music.

Bad sex is a choice.

I was nineteen when I realized that, and it changed my life. I was dating this guy named Aaron, who had a very detailed list of the things he liked in bed — pegging, doggy, reverse cowgirl, never missionary. Fucking him was a goddamn workout, so at least he saved me money on a gym membership. He never failed to come his brains out, but I was not so lucky.

I'd had okay sex with everyone I'd fucked before Aaron, and I couldn't understand what was happening with him. It was only after he dumped me three months into our relationship and his frat brother, Joachim, helped me get over him that I realized my mistake. Aaron had a very detailed list of the things he wanted in bed, but he'd never asked me what I wanted, and I was too naïve to know that I could give him my sexual rider in the same way he'd given me his.

The lesson I learned during the Thanksgiving break I spent in Joachim's bed was that telling the people you fucked what you like wasn't just a good idea, it was necessary, and it could be sexy as fuck. I appreciate Joachim's guidance on this issue. I have never fucked anyone with a filthier mouth, and I know his wives are happy as hell. Alfonso isn't nearly as expressive, but he gives good talk when it counts.

"Give it to me," he groans. "Put all your weight on me. Fuck, I need to feel it."

He says some other stuff too, but it's all in Italian. I can guess at the translations by the way his big, rough hands take hold of my hips, and his lap lifts to meet mine. By the time our bodies are slapping loudly together, words don't matter anyway, I think. I'm wrong.

"Yes, fuck her. Fuck her. My God."

We both freeze at those words.

Without the noise we were making, the garden is quiet enough that we can hear the sound of skin rubbing against skin.

When we turn around, we see the man from the pool, standing out in the path, watching us, his pants around his knees and his dick in his hands.

Now, I have done some wild shit, but something about this feels like a bit much, even for me. Maybe it's the fact that he's not trying to hide at all. Or the fact that he found us. Went looking for us? Or the fact that I'm into it — still clenching my pussy around Alfonso's dick into it. And apparently, I'm not alone.

Alfonso's hips are shifting up to get deeper inside me. "Please," he groans after a while of me crouching above him.

I turn back and grip his shoulders harder to keep myself steady. "Are you...are you sure?" I ask giddily.

He unbuttons his shirt and nudges my hand inside. And

then he nods and begins to move his hips again. "Make it hurt."

Like I said, he's not a man of many words, but he damn sure knows how to pick the good ones.

I dig my fingernails into his shoulders as I start to fuck him again.

I let him move me when he needs to, rocking me back and forth and side to side and in a circle because we both want him to hit every inch of me.

I scratch a new piece of skin whenever he hits a spot I particularly like.

We keep our eyes on one another while we begin to fuck loudly. Sometimes the sounds of our anonymous friend getting off watching us cut through the noises we're making, but mostly it's just Alfonso and me fucking like fat, happy rabbits.

It would have been nice to come together; that was a thing Tyrone, Kevin, and I had mastered, which was no small feat. But this moment is not the last two years I spent with my exes, and that's okay.

Our friend comes first. By the time he's close, his Australian accent is nearly incomprehensible, but somehow, I guess that it's nothing but obscenities as he beats the ever-loving shit out of his dick. He moans so loudly I think he's dying, but that's his business.

Alfonso and I are close. We're groaning into one another's mouths. I'm sucking his tongue. And he's practically slamming my hips into his.

I wrap my right arm around his neck so I can get the angle right, and then I snake my fingers between our bodies to play with my clit. It only takes a few hard brushes before

I'm coming so hard that the sound of our bodies is wetter than before, our sweat and my orgasm mixing together.

But I don't want to come alone if I don't have to. So, once the first wave of my orgasm rips through me, I release Alfonso's tongue and then sink my teeth into his bottom lip.

He cries out and then pumps up desperately, his ass lifting from the bench and then freezing as he jerks inside of me.

I don't let his lip go until his body relaxes, and then I soothe it with gentle swipes of my tongue.

We're not in a rush to leave one another.

Alfonso holds me close, petting my hips and placing soft kisses on my lips.

Eventually, we hear the sound of the man zipping up his pants and walking slowly, casually away.

"Did you like that?" he asks.

"Don't ask foolish questions," I tell him. "Your lap is full of the answer."

I like the way his laughter feels against my mouth.

I WAKE up to a pulsing ache everywhere.

My legs, my arms, my back, my lips. This isn't the first time I've woken up this way, but it is the first time it's ever felt this good. I feel like one big throbbing nerve. I blink awake, and all the blood in my body begins to pound as if it was waiting for me to regain consciousness so I can take full advantage of these new sensations.

The circular bite marks Zoe left in the meat of my thighs while she was using her hands and mouth on me. The slightly jagged scratches her fingernails made across my back, the wounds she gave me while I was grinding into her. And my lips, sore not just from her bite but all of the hours we spent kissing. I've never had a night like last night before, and I wake up with a hard cock and a numb arm because Zoe's been using it as a pillow. I just add the tingling numbness to the rest of the things I'm feeling.

I smile up at the ceiling while I listen to the soft sounds of her sleeping. Not for nothing, but I think I could stay here all day, so of course, Nicola ruins it.

There's a knock on the door, and I know it's my brother. I spent my entire childhood being interrupted by him like this. Still, I don't rush getting out of the bed. I take my time replacing my arm with a pillow underneath Zoe's head, making sure not to disturb her sleep. I grab a towel that one of us — I don't even remember who — threw there after a midnight dip in the pool. I hold it up against my groin and open the door, only just enough to glare at my brother.

There's an annoying smile on his face already.

"Buongiorno. Comè e andata la tua serata?" He laughs loudly. "Cosa è successso al tuo labbro?"

"What do you want?" I hiss.

"Oh, I guess that means it was good," he says, snaking his hand through the door and tapping at my shoulder.

I hiss when his fingers hit at the edges of one of Zoe's wounds. That stinging pain isn't the same as when she gave it to me. I shift away from his hand. "What do you want?" I ask again, this time through clenched teeth.

Nicola laughs, the piece of shit. "We need to go. Fast." He looks as serious as he can.

"Nicola, what did you—"

He shakes his head sharply and cuts me off. "We can fight on the boat. Wake up my sister, and let's go. Fifteen minutes."

"Va fanculo," I say.

"I'd tell you to do the same, but it seems as if Zoe took care of that. Buongiorno, sorella."

"Good morning, Nicola. Are we making an escape?" she asks and then yawns.

I can't turn around to look at her, not with Nicola here.

"Si, si. Just a little escape. But quick, no?"

She yawns again. "Okay."

Nicola turns to me with a wink. "I like her more than you."

I slam the door in his face.

Zoe

I don't enjoy the boat ride back to Positano nearly as much because I sleep through it. But Alfonso does let me use his lap as a pillow, so I can't say that I *don't* enjoy it; it's just not the same kind of luxury sunbathing.

When we make it to Positano, there's a line to get to the pier, and while we wait, Alfonso goes to the cockpit to argue with Nicola. I'm nosy, so I rest my chin on my hands and boldly watch them while I'm only half awake.

They're too engrossed in their argument to notice. Eventually, though, Nicola needs to focus on pulling alongside the pier, so he dismisses Alfonso with a sharp cut of his hand in the air, and I hear Alfonso grunt something in Italian as he comes back.

"We're here," he says in a surprisingly gentle voice.

"What were you fighting about?"

He picks the duffel bag of our clothes up and throws it over his shoulder. "Our shared ignorance," he says nonchalantly and extends his hand to help me from the bench.

"Wanna share any details?" I ask as if I'm interviewing one of my subjects.

"No."

Nicola pulls the boat along the pier, and then he and

Alfonso help me off of the yacht. I grab the bag, and before we leave, Alfonso turns to his brother, and they hug, tight and fierce. They kiss one another on each cheek, and Alfonso climbs onto the pier and takes the bag from my hand.

Nicola waves at me. "I'll see you next time, sorella, si? He always comes home for Christmas."

"No, I don't," Alfonso groans.

Nicola is walking back toward the cockpit. "He should. Make him."

Alfonso sighs and leads me down the pier toward the beach.

"So, what's he smuggling?" I ask nonchalantly.

Alfonso looks at me and laughs. "Is it that obvious?"

I shrug. "He has a boat. He's a little too mysterious. Yes, it's that obvious."

We walk down a set of stone steps to the beach and trudge through the sand toward the town. "I don't know what he's moving or for whom. That's what we were fighting about."

"Ah. Got it."

"Is there anything else you would like to know?" he asks, smiling warmly at me. His bottom lip is very red and a little bruised, but he looks relaxed in a way I haven't seen him in the three days of our whirlwind acquaintance.

"Do I have to walk up those fucking steps?"

"Yes."

I lean toward him. "Are you in pain?"

I watch a shudder run through his body. He swallows loudly. I enjoy the way he's expressly avoiding looking at me, even though his face is turning red. "Yes."

"Good."

I'm not looking forward to the stairs again, but if I can tease Alfonso and myself, I think it'll be worth it. I'm smiling like a cat who got the cream at Alfonso, so I see the moment that his heated embarrassment changes and hardens. I watch as he stops being someone who can feel the scratches I left on his back and becomes someone who'll punch another man's face into a bag of broken bones and blood like he did the day we met.

"What's wrong?" I whisper.

He doesn't answer. He grabs my hand and practically pulls me to the street. He's walking faster now, obliterating all hope that we aren't in trouble. He's too focused for me to ask if this is Nicola's trouble wearing off on us or if whatever we've been running from has finally arrived from Naples.

MY MOTHER once told me everything I touch turns to ashes.

I remember that day like it was yesterday. Of course, I remember the way her face crumpled and the tears that ran down her cheeks when she realized what she said. I know she regretted it, but I still remember those words.

I remember how I felt when I heard them; how they answered some question about who I was that had been hiding deep inside me. I hadn't understood who I was before my mother told me, and after that, I hadn't been able to think of myself in any other way. So, of course, I hear her voice when I see Andrea Fanulli prowling around the beach.

I recognize him from the amateur boxing league that I sometimes visit. I told Giulio I went to scout new talent, but now I know it's because I needed the hit. Literally. I needed the shot of adrenaline from a fist hitting my jaw and making my teeth rattle. I needed the sting of split skin and bone against bone and blood flowing into my eyes.

Andrea always fought like poverty was biting at his heels, and he has that hungry look in his eyes when I see him today as if when he finds me, he's going to swallow me whole. Knowing him, I think he'll try.

He won't succeed, but that's not the point. I don't want him coming at me while I have Zoe by my side.

"Stay here," I tell her.

I step into the Russos' grocery, a place where I practically grew up, and see Giovanni. "Prestami il tuo scooter," I bark at him.

"Hey," Zoe calls to me. "Be nice."

I roll my eyes and turn back to Giovanni. "Per favore," I say and then glance over my shoulder at her.

She nods.

Giovanni hands his keys over the counter. "È tua moglie?"

"Stai zitto," I hiss and stomp back to Zoe.

We have to walk up the road to a bank of scooters parked along the side of the road. Giovanni's scooter is all black with red rims. I was there when he painted them.

I throw my leg over the bike and then turn to Zoe, nodding to the backseat. She's clutching our duffel bag to her chest, looking at me with wide eyes. "What's happening?" she asks in a fluttering wisp of a voice that makes my heart and dick throb.

"Whoever is coming for Salvo has found us. Let me get you somewhere safe." I see her arms tighten around the bag. She looks left and right, her eyes wide with fear. "Solarità, per favore. Please."

She looks at me with big, vulnerable, wet eyes. "Okay." And then she climbs onto Giovanni's scooter, the bag pressed between her front and my back. Her arms are wrapped around me. "Okay," she whispers against my neck.

"Okay."

"It's not better on the way down. I cannot believe this."

Zoe complains every step of the way to my parents' home. I would complain right back at her, but I'm preoccupied, and I use her whining just to confirm that she is alright.

The relief I feel when we enter the family garden is too much to even enumerate.

"Zoe, mi amore. Bentornate. Bentornate."

"Welcome," I tell her.

"Yeah, I figured," she says, just before my mother pulls her down into a hug.

I want to stay here. In a perfect world, I could stay in this space where my mother is happy that I've returned home but doesn't feel the need to ask me more than a question or two. But I do not live in a perfect world. I live in a world where Zoe is still grasping at the bag of our clothes. Where my mother is murmuring to her in an Italian that Zoe cannot understand that everything will be alright, even though she doesn't know that for certain. I exist in a world where Ugo is watching me with hard eyes. This is a world where I have to leave Zoe without any assurances that I'll return. That would be cruel.

"WHERE HAVE YOU BEEN?" my mother scolds us as she walks Zoe toward the house. "I sent Ugo to invite you for dinner, but he said you were gone."

She resumes her seat at the small round table in the shade. There's a bowl of peas on the tabletop that she's shucking. She smiles at me lovingly in a way I haven't seen since I was very young. I know this smile. She wants to let me know how much she likes Zoe, and I hate how much I want to bask in her approval.

"We went to Capri with Nicola," I tell her.

"Oh, that's nice. A little early honeymoon. Your brother needs help with the tomatoes. Go wash your hands."

"Not today, mamma," I say as gently as I can.

She turns at my voice and squints. "What's wrong?"

I shake my head quickly. I can see by the way she frowns that she knows I'm lying. She always does. My mother is the reason why I don't bother to lie. But I can't tell her what's really happening, so I keep moving forward. "I have to meet an associate in Sorrento. I'll be back tomorrow. Can Zoe stay here?"

I feel Zoe pull her hand from mine, and my mother sees it as well. But I can't worry about that right now. I don't have time. I don't know if Andrea saw me on the beach, but if he gets a clue and begins to ask around, I won't be hard to find. Good. I'm more than ready to know what's going on and who is coming for Salvo. All that matters is that Andrea doesn't find me here or get anywhere close to my family and Zoe.

I can't tell my mother any of this, so I focus on her face, communicating the urgency of my emotions, if nothing else. And I will give her this — whatever she thinks I do for a living, and however she feels about that, I am still her son.

She nods and turns to Zoe. "Do you know how to..." She looks at me in confusion. "Sguciare. What's the English?"

"Shuck," I tell her.

She recoils. "Ugly. Come, Zoe. I'll teach you."

I have to turn to her now, and I wish I didn't. Just an hour ago, Zoe's eyes were big and bright and playful, even if a little tired. It was the perfect combination. If given the chance, I would want to see her like that every day for as long as she'll keep me around. But now, she's looking at me with wariness in her eyes. And questions. So many questions. But I can't give her answers. Not right now, not in front of my mother. I try to apologize for that without words. I want to explain that I'll tell her everything when this is all over, but unlike my mother, Zoe hasn't spent years studying my face. She can't pick out the messages I'm trying to broadcast. All she has is fear and confusion, and I wish I was leaving her with better memories of me.

"I'm sorry," I tell her. "I'll be back soon."

She opens her mouth to say something — probably something I would prefer that she not — and I brace myself for whatever is coming, but there's nothing. She rolls her eyes and then plasters a big fake smile on her face before she turns to my mother.

"Can I just watch?" she asks carefully.

My mother laughs. "Sfacciata," she says, pushing the bowl of peas toward Zoe.

I watch them for a few seconds before my mother shoos me away. "Go to your meeting," she says. "Zoe will be fine here, with me. She'll be a perfect Italian housewife by the time you return."

Zoe's laughter is beautiful but sad.

I want to tell her that I can't think of anything I would like less. I don't know her well, but I like her exactly as she is. Unfortunately, that's yet another thing I shouldn't say in front of my mother, so I grab her shoulder tenderly and squeeze.

Before I leave, I duck around the back of the house and find Ugo sorting the tomatoes he's harvested.

"Wash your hands," he says as soon as I'm close.

"I'm not here to help," I tell him.

"You never are."

I ignore that. "I need you to do something for me."

He looks up at that. I never ask for help.

"Zoe's with mamma. I need to go..." I think about explaining, but I don't. With mamma, I didn't want to confirm her worst suspicions of me, and with Ugo, I don't want to mar the simplicity of the life he loves, the life he's created here, stepping onto the path my parents and our grandparents carved with their own hands into this mountain. "I need to go. If I'm not back by tomorrow afternoon, I need you to take Zoe to Nicola and have him take her to Naples. And tell Nicola that he needs to contact Giulio."

"And who's Giulio?"

"Nicola knows. All you have to do is get her to him and let him take it from there. Please."

"Why wouldn't you come back?"

I reach out and grab my brother's face. "Don't worry about it, okay? This is only a precaution. Will you do this for me?"

He nods, but I can see the skepticism in his eyes.

"Thank you," I say and then kiss his cheeks.

I turn away, ready to leave. Every step I take away from Ugo, I become less like the brother he knows and more like the monster I can be.

"Stai attento," he calls to me. My steps falter for a second, but I don't turn back.

Careful isn't something I'm normally good at. Certainly, Ugo has never said that to me before. But on my way out of my parents' garden, I hear Zoe and my mother laughing with one another, and I think that maybe I can try to exercise a little caution for once in my life.

I RETURN Giovanni's scooter and then attach myself to a crowd of tourists heading toward the shore. Once I'm there, I duck into a restaurant so I can scan the beach while I pull out my mobile phone.

Giulio answers on the first ring. Always a bad sign.

"Where are you?" he asks.

"Exactly where I'm supposed to be."

"Good. I need you to come back."

"When?"

"As soon as you can."

"I have some unexpected visitors," I tell him. "I might not be able to get away until tomorrow."

He grunts. I can hear his jaw working; it clicks sometimes when he grinds his teeth, which is very rare. Also not a good sign.

I think I see someone who looks like Andrea, and I move to another window, but it's not him.

"I've been trying to contact my parents, but they haven't been answering." Both of his parents were dead long before we met, so I know who he's talking about. I wonder if he's told Zahra this. I wonder if I should tell Zoe. I wonder if I'll get the chance. "When you get here, we'll take a trip. As soon as your guests leave—"

"I understand."

Giulio grunts, which is as close as we usually come to saying goodbye, but I stop him.

"Should I come alone, or can I bring a friend?"

"A friend?" Giulio asks.

"Yes."

He laughs before disconnecting the call, but I think I hear him yell to Zahra, "Hai vinto alla lotteria, amore."

I consider calling him back, but then I catch a glimpse of someone who doesn't seem to fit in with the crowds of tourists, and I follow him with my eyes. I haven't lived in Positano for years, but I don't recognize this man as a local. So, I shove my phone back into the pocket of my shorts and follow him.

Zoe

I like Maria, but she was not playing about making me into a housewife. For the rest of the afternoon, she puts me to *work*. We shuck peas and pick lettuce. We make pasta, and then she tries to teach me how to make pesto from scratch. Once again, I refuse to commit anything she's saying to memory, but I'll never forget the smell of the fresh bread in her oven or the vegetables her husband is grilling outside. I'm pissed at Alfonso, but at least his mother feeds me well.

We're just sitting down for lunch when the gate squeaks, and Ugo says something to his father with a sigh and shake of his head. His father pats his arm and says in simple, halting English for my benefit, "You can fix the gate later."

"I thought he just fixed the gate?" Dario asks.

All of a sudden, Maria is pure movement, getting up from the table to get another plate for her favorite son and setting a place for him next to me. Dario kisses his father's cheek, his brother's, his mother's, and then sits, turning to me. "May I, sorella?"

He doesn't say that word in the same way Nicola did, playful but warm. Dario says 'sorella' like an accusation as if he's waiting to catch me in a very obvious lie. And not for nothing, but I don't give a shit if a priest thinks I'm lying. I'm pissed enough at Alfonso for leaving me here without a damn explanation that I don't care about blowing up his spot right now either. But Maria and Gabriele have been so lovely to me, and the last thing I want to do is disrespect their hospitality.

So, I give Dario my fakest smile and offer him my left cheek. "Certo," I whisper.

Maria claps like I've given a speech in Italian, and I know that I've made the right decision. Dario kisses my cheek in a brief, glancing brush, and then we get to the business of eating.

Thank God.

I'm lounging in the shade of a bread lemon tree for the riposo.

I mean, I'm also hiding from Maria because while we were clearing the plates, she said something about teaching me how to bake some dessert I can't even pronounce. I've been ducking and dodging my mother's efforts to teach me how to make cake since I was twelve. I like Maria, but not enough to go against my morals.

Besides, after a lunch of nothing but delicious carbs and a small glass of something called grappa with Gabriele, I'm done for. I'm ready for a cute little nap, especially after last night. But I don't want to think about last night or Alfonso, especially when all my toys are over two hundred steps away. I'm a mixture of sleepy and grumpy, and Dario appearing does nothing for my mood.

"How are you, sorella?"

"I'm fine," I say, stretching my legs out on the bench so he'll sit somewhere else or maybe even leave. I hope he leaves.

He does not. "Where is my brother?" he asks. "I can't believe he left your side."

"I don't like clingy men."

He looks deep into my eyes, trying to catch me in a lie, but of all the things I have no problem lying about, this is not one. Clingy men and arrogant assholes are two types of men I will not be expending any time or energy entertaining, and I'm beginning to suspect that Dario might be the latter. I think Dario begins to realize that he's not my favorite brother because he takes a seat on a tree stump stool and changes tactics.

"I love my brother," he says.

I don't answer because while I like Alfonso a lot and I have a real affinity for his thick thighs after last night, I certainly do not love him. I could, though — maybe — and that thought shocks the shit out of me. Still, I think it's best to keep my trap shut.

When I don't answer, Dario keeps going. "He isn't always the easiest person to love. He doesn't always do the right thing. Sometimes he doesn't even know what the right thing is," he says. "But he's a good person when you dig past his rough exterior."

That rubs me all the way wrong, and I decide to tell him so. "Shut up," I spit out. "Alfonso doesn't have a rough exterior."

Clearly, no one has told Dario about himself in a long time because he sits up straight, and his mouth falls open in shock.

"I don't know where you get off talking about him like that, but I'd appreciate it if you kept your poor opinion of your *brother* to yourself." I have a lot of feelings about Zahra and Shae's recent decisions — and I plan to tell them each and every one of my thoughts when I see them again — but I wouldn't let someone talk bad about them to me, and I certainly wouldn't trash them to a stranger. Not like this.

"I love my brother," Dario says again.

"Then act like it," I spit back.

"Dario," Maria says.

She's appeared out of nowhere, and I sit up straight. Dario stands and turns to his mother.

"Will you take this to Carlotta?" she says, handing him a bag that I'm sure is full of more of her leftovers. In my mind,

I imagine that her food is sustaining this entire valley, and that makes me like her all the more.

"Of course, mamma," Dario says.

He takes the bag from her and kisses her cheek. He turns back to me and smiles. I don't return the gesture.

When he's gone, Maria comes and sits next to me on the bench. There are birds chirping and a dog barking somewhere. I've been told it's Ugo's, but I haven't seen him yet.

"I think you will be good for my son," Maria says.

That sentence makes me feel surprisingly sad. If... No, *when* Alfonso returns, eventually, he'll take me back to Naples. I'm going to see Zahra and speak to her, but in the end, if I have to, I'll leave Italy without them. Alfonso was right; my sister and cousin are grown women, and if they want to stay here with these men, they can. They deserve to be happy.

I'll leave here, and I'll never see Maria again, and I feel bad that she thinks this is only the beginning. "Maria," I say, my mind scrambling for how to open the door to let her down gently. "Alfonso says that you want grandchildren," I start.

Her face brightens, and she grins at me with Alfonso's smile. "Si, si, si."

I take a deep breath and frown at her. "I don't know how to tell you this, but I... I don't want to have any children."

Her face falls. "Is it...?" She reaches out and pats my stomach. It's a little rude but also kind of endearing. "Is something wrong?" she asks.

"No," I tell her gently. "I've just never wanted kids."

Now she's frowning sadly. "And Alfonso knows this?"

I nod slowly.

She turns and looks out across the gardens, and I do the same. We sit in more silence until I feel Maria shrug.

"Okay," she says in a surprisingly bright tone. "I still have two others."

I turn to her with a laugh. "Maria?"

She grins at me again. "Alfonso has never done what I want. He's..." She takes a few seconds to think of the word. "Asino."

"Huh?"

She's still thinking when Ugo comes into our line of view with a basket of more produce. Maria calls to him in Italian.

"Donkey," he calls back.

Maria shakes her head and yells at him again. I hear Alfonso's name.

Ugo drops the basket in the shade near the front door of the house, and then he turns to head back into a greenhouse at the edge of the property. He laughs. "Jackass," he calls to his mother. "He's stubborn."

"Yes. Yes," she says, turning back to me. "My boy is stubborn. He was almost two weeks late being born! But you are right," she tells me, reaching for my hands. "He is a good boy just as he is. And if the two of you do not want babies, then I will be okay with that. But maybe you can bring Alfonso home more often. Yes, that you can do." She smiles triumphantly at me, and I have to laugh.

"You and my mother would get along very well."

"Oh, good. I cannot wait to meet her."

GIULIO LIKES to skulk in the shadows with his guns.

That works for him, and the brooding, sad orphan thing got him Zahra, but it's not an option for me. I'm too big and tall and noticeable on any day, anywhere, but especially here where most people don't just notice me; they've known my family for generations. It makes it difficult to stalk this man, who I'm certain is here to find me.

Difficult, but not impossible. I trail him from the beach into the main shopping plaza. I use the crowd to hide me as best I can, but I keep my distance. I don't have to track him far. There's a fountain in the center of the plaza where I spy Andrea and another man. I peel off into a leather shop.

"Alfonso," Signora Galicia calls to me.

I greet her and let her pull me into the store. I keep one eye on the cluster of Andrea and his men while I listen to Signora Galicia's story about this past winter — she spent it in Puglia with her son. When Andrea and his men begin to move, I make my apologies to the Signora and follow them. They're heading back to the beach, but that's not ideal.

"Andrea," I call out.

He turns at his name. I wave and then duck into an alley. They're smart enough not to run and gather unwanted attention. I use that to my advantage.

There's a dry riverbed that runs down the length of the mountain from Montepertuso to Positano. Most tourists never notice it, but locals sometimes cut through here when they're in a hurry to catch a ferry. It's a surprisingly secluded place to hide, right on the edge of the busy town center.

Here, I am in my element.

They should have brought guns. I would have. I've never had to face someone as big as me, but I know that whenever that day comes, I don't plan to waste my time or energy trying to fight him hand to hand.

I like pain, but I do not have a death wish.

Apparently, Andrea does.

Maybe it's the prestige. Maybe he wants to be able to tell everyone that he fought me and won. Either way, arrogance is deadly.

Andrea moves toward me, pulling his shirt over his head. His men stand sentry at the mouth of the cave, blocking my path, foolishly assuming I plan to run away when I never have before.

"Who sent you?" I ask, pushing the sleeves of my shirt up my arms.

"That's none of your business," he says.

I roll my shoulders in a circle, and the scratches Zoe left

all over my back sting, reminding me of her. As if I could forget. "You can tell me now, or you can tell me when you have barely any teeth left in your mouth."

Andrea laughs mirthlessly, but I see one of his men flinch at the promise because that's what I've made to him. We all know what I can do.

"You'll be dead before that," he says.

"If you came here to kill me, you should have done it already."

Andrea shrugs. "Of course, I came here to kill you, but I want to give you a chance to fight for your life," he says. "I think it will be fun."

I've met a lot of sadistic bastards. Some might say that I'm one of them. So, I know what terrifying looks like. It's not Andrea.

"Do they know who sent you? Or can I kill them first?"

They shift again, and Andrea frowns, but he doesn't give me an answer, which is all the answer I need.

I've watched enough of Andrea's fights to know that his left side is his weakness. Not every fighter can be ambidextrous, but it helps to shore up your non-dominant side, a lesson I know Andrea's manager told him often enough. A lesson I know he's yet to learn when my fist collides with his jaw.

That crack of bone and flesh is like a gunshot in this cave, and it gets my blood roaring.

If I had wanted to kill him with one punch, I could have, but I don't. I stun him, and he falls to the ground. I turn on his associates. They're frozen in place at the shocking turn of events, and I take advantage, which — besides pain — is one of my other skills.

It takes an unfortunately small amount of work to beat them unconscious. When I turn back to Andrea, he's standing but dazed, and there's a knife in his hand.

"At least you're not a complete idiot," I say, lunging for him.

I feel his blade slice through my shirt and skin. I don't care. Those petty cuts are nothing compared to my knuckles connecting with his face, his teeth cracking and slicing up his mouth, the warm rush of his blood and spittle running over my fists.

I feel like myself again as I punch him repeatedly, breaking his teeth, his nose, his cheeks, his orbital bones. Everything. His face swells, and I keep punching, feeling the wet sack of blood and bone fragments under his swollen skin. I hit him until my shoulders and hands ache. Until Zoe's scratches become one wide, pulsing wound. Until Andrea drops the knife and begins to beg — in wet, bloody bubbles — for his life.

"I'll tell you," he says. "I'll tell you."

I stop and wait.

"It was the Serpente Nero," he says. "They sent me."

"Ovviamente lo era," I hiss. "Why didn't I think of that?"

And then, because I'm merciful, I snap Andrea's neck. Now he doesn't have to explain what happened to his face. Besides, we both know the Serpente would have done much worse than that once they found out he'd failed.

My first call is to Nicola.

My second is to Giulio.

The call I want to make is home. Where Zoe is. But that will have to wait.

BEFORE DINNER, Ugo hiked down to Nicola's house for my suitcase. He gave it to me with a kind grunt.

After dinner, I tell Maria that I'm tired and retreat to the bedroom where she's set me up to be alone. I dig my cell phone out of my purse and cringe at all of the missed messages. My mother has sent me novella-length emails wondering where in the hell Zahra is. KeKe sent messages asking how I was liking Positano and then why I hadn't moved in over a day. I have to respond to her messages quickly because I know my best friend, and I don't want her to alert Interpol.

I avoid all the other messages from my editor and friends and begin to type a very long email to Tyrone and Kevin. A few days ago, I thought this email would have been hard to write; too many emotions to sort into coherent sentences, too many things we'd left unsaid for so long that it had rent us apart. Too many dreams we'd pulled from whole cloth where we imagined our relationship heading somewhere else.

When we fought that night, not even a week ago, I'd accused them of trying to trap me, but in the cooling darkness of Maria and Gabriele's house in the Positano mountains, after all the chaotic randomness of the last few days, I can finally admit that I had let them believe that something was possible, even if only in my silences.

On our first date, they told me that they wanted children. I told them that babies weren't part of my current life plan when I should have said that they never would be. So, I guess I do have something to apologize for after all.

I apologize for not ending it there, for laughing nervously when they mentioned kids after that rather than shutting it down, for staying and letting us all believe that we could change one another.

It wasn't all me, but I don't bother trying to convince them of that. There's no point, and we're well past the moment in our relationship where any of that mattered.

"I just wanted you to know that I loved you, but love isn't nearly enough. I'm sorry we had to realize that together."

I press send without proofreading because I know what I'm like. If I let myself read over my words, I'll overthink them, revise each paragraph, soften the strength of what I need to say. I'll try to fix what isn't broken, just over. I'll start blaming them in the same sentence where I ask for their forgiveness. I'll make a fool of myself and shit all over a relationship that was actually beautiful for most of the time the three of us were together, and I don't want that. I don't want them to think less of me in their memories because I won't think less of them; I've spent a lot of the last few days trying.

Once the email is sent, I toss my phone on the bed and then head outside.

I hear a television behind Maria and Gabriele's bedroom door as I pass. I know Ugo is resting in his small renovated shack, but I still expect to see him digging in the dirt when I step outside.

But the garden is empty, and the scent of flowers is so strong that the air feels thick. It's cooler out here than it was in the afternoon, thankfully. Barefoot, I carefully pick my way through rows of lettuces, my eyes on the midnight blue sky. At the edge of the property, I can see the sea through the trees. I smile, imagining Nicola doing some criminal shit on that water. It looks like smooth, dark velvet, and it reminds me of that alcove on Capri.

And then I think about Alfonso. It would be a lie to say that I don't want to think about him because I do. But I don't want to wonder where he is, what he's doing, or if he's in danger — I'm sure he is — and I hate that. I hate that I barely know this man, but he has me worrying like some mob girlfriend. I know his dick was good but was it that good?

Unfortunately, the answer is yes.

I'm fighting with myself, trying to only make room for good thoughts in my mind — like the way his blunt fingers had felt inside me just twenty-four hours ago — rather than picturing him bloody and bruised at the bottom of a long flight of stone steps.

The gate creaks open.

At first, I think it's Ugo. Maybe he went out for a drink.

Or maybe he has a girlfriend up a few hundred steps that he visits after his parents fall asleep. Or maybe it's Nicola or Dario — that last thought makes me angry.

But it's Alfonso who comes ambling into the garden. I don't know him well enough to recognize his tall, hulking frame in shadow, or I shouldn't. But as it turns out, I do. He's walking slowly toward the house, and instead of calling out to him, I mirror his steps, still picking carefully through the rows of lettuce. I don't want to mess up Ugo and Gabriele's hard work.

He's almost at the house before he notices me.

He goes still and turns in my direction. "What are you doing out here?" he asks.

"I couldn't sleep," I say. We both know that's a lie. "I was worried you wouldn't come back." Even if I wanted to hide the truth of those words, I couldn't. My breath hitches, and my mouth has gone dry.

Alfonso's face is covered in shadow and specks of blood or dirt or both.

I stop, stepping carefully around Ugo's vegetables. "What the fuck happened to you?"

He laughs softly. "This is nothing," he says. "Believe me."

Sadly, I do.

We're standing in front of one another, and even in the dim light, I can see that whatever the fuck Alfonso left here to do, he did, and he paid a price, but someone else paid more.

"Jesus, Alfonso," I say, squinting at him. "I'll ask your mother if she has—"

He places a hand over my stomach. "Don't. I don't want her to see me like this."

There's so much left unsaid in those words, and I want to tell him that his mother knows who he is, but I understand. She might know who he is, but knowing and seeing are two different things.

"Okay," I whisper. "But we should clean you up."

He tips his head toward the greenhouse, and I begin to turn. His hand settles on my back as we walk.

"Ugo's in the shed," I say. Alfonso holds fast to my waist, and we walk toward the greenhouse. Eventually, I see why.

There's a showerhead bolted to the side of an old brick building and a slab of concrete on the ground.

"Ugo put this shower up a few years ago," he says while reaching around me to turn the spigot.

"Okay."

His hands grip my hips, and his mouth brushes my ear. "I wanted to come back to you," he says.

And that's the moment I realize that I've gotten over Tyrone and Kevin.

Alfonso

Every part of me hurts or stings or twinges.

There's almost no space on my body that isn't on fire with a cut or scratch or the imprint of Zoe's bite.

I could spend weeks enjoying the sensations of these

wounds. The heat of fresh lacerations. The itchy burning of a healing injury. The scars.

But it's all different with Zoe.

She helps me carefully peel my clothes off. Her fingers graze the jagged scratches and bites she gave me and the neat slices from Andrea's knife. She's carefully careless with me, enjoying the way I flinch and groan at her touch.

And then her hands flatten against my back, and she pushes me under the spray.

I moan so loudly that I can swear it echoes across the valley.

This is a shower Ugo made for utility, but with Zoe, it feels luxurious. Water drips down my body as I watch her undress for me. I want to turn up the light from the moon, so I can see every inch of her, the soft curves of her hips, the gentle hang of her large breasts, the dimples on her thighs, and the beautiful bulge of her stomach. I want to drink Zoe in, but she hasn't given me permission yet.

So, I wait.

Zoe finds the soap Ugo leaves out here. It's antiseptic for the errant cuts and harsh lye, so he doesn't have to linger under this spray that never gets higher than tepid. I watch her soap her hands and then her body. I suck in a harsh breath as she walks toward me. I brace myself for the sting of the soap, her touch, her body. Her.

"Si, Dio, si. Si."

Zoe uses her hands and her curves to clean me. She presses herself against me, rubbing me up and down and down and up. It takes no time at all before I'm a shuddering mess, my cock heavy and hard between my legs, my hips grinding into any part of her body I can reach, my hand grasping at her ass. My lips move against her ear, her cheek, her neck, begging her to give me more. Pleading with her to let me give her everything.

She pushes me against the wall. The old brick hits her scratches, and I cry out. I call her name.

I watch Zoe walk slowly under the spray, her big curly hair flattening against her head. She presses her body against me, and I grab her, holding her close.

"I'm on birth control," she says and then turns around.

"What? Oh, God."

Zoe drags her hip along the length of my dick, squeezing it between her body and mine. I cry out in a desperate wail and then bash the back of my head against the hard brick. Zoe bends forward, reaches between her legs, and then presses me against her opening.

"Sisisi," I hiss as Zoe pushes back and lets me sink inside her hot, wet cunt.

This is what it feels like to be home.

Zoe

I don't know if it's the heightened emotions or the cool night air or the damn near cold water, but this is the best sex of my life.

I don't have a list ranking all of my lovers anymore, but if I did, Alfonso would be top of it right now. There's something about feeling his fat, veiny dick inside of me with nothing between us, his hard, rounded stomach hitting my ass, or his beefy fingers digging into my hips, but I come with only a few strokes, the fear of the last few hours amplifying every slap of our bodies joining together again.

I don't stop fucking back into him. I fuck Alfonso at my own pace, as hard and as soft as I like. He doesn't ask me for anything more than all of me, and he doesn't rush my climax. All Alfonso does is flinch against the brick digging into his skin and cry my name at higher and higher notes.

And just like last night, we lose control. We're rutting against each other. I'm throwing it back hard enough to hurt. And I know it hurts because Alfonso is cursing and crying in Italian, too far gone to remember English.

I did that. My pussy did that. The thought makes me come a second time. And then again. And then again.

"I'm close," Alfonso groans. "I'm coming."

I pull away from him, just enough to feel his dick pop free.

He groans sadly.

I turn around and shut off the water. "Make yourself come," I tell him. "I want you to come on me."

The sounds of nature – nightbirds chirping, insects, water flowing - are interrupted by the fast, wet, desperate slap of Alfonso's fist fucking his dick. I let him shove his other hand between my legs and circle my clit while he gets himself off. And when he's close, when he's shuddering with every stroke, I pull him toward me, he buries his face in my neck, and then I cup his balls right before he empties them onto my belly.

"Cazzo. Cazzo. Ti amo."

We catch our breaths and then wash the remnants of sweat and blood and come from our bodies. We slip into the house and then squash together in his childhood bed, which was probably too small for him more than a decade ago. I don't tell him that I love him because I don't. And I don't ask him if he meant it because I know he did.

But I do hold him close because it's only a matter of time.

ALL OF ME HURTS. I'm sore. I'm tired. I would like to sleep for another twenty hours at least. There are parts of my body I've never consciously thought about that are throbbing right now, and I am very aware of those muscles and tendons and Alfonso's mouth brushing against them.

I wake up to his mouth on me, first my shoulders, then across my back, then down my spine. He pushes me onto my stomach and continues to kiss down my body.

"Fuck," I whisper into the pillow.

He crawls down the bed, down my body, never losing contact with my skin. He places kisses along the broad width of my hips and around each buttock.

"Yes."

He pushes my left leg up onto the bed with one hand while the other spreads my thighs. And then both hands are on my ass, spreading my cheeks.

"Fuck yes," I groan as Alfonso's tongue travels down the crack of my ass, circling my asshole lightly and then licking at my pussy.

I scream as quietly as I can into the pillow as he teases me from my clit to my pussy to my ass and back again. He laughs against my lips as he laps at me.

"Oh my God." I dig my nails into the mattress.

Alfonso's body is a map of contradictions. Soft tongue, rough palms. Slow strokes, pounding hips. Hard dick and the softest, sweetest words. He pushes me up to my knees, ass in the air. He's let me take the lead since the day we met, but it feels good to give over just a bit of control for the moment, especially when Alfonso takes such good care of my pussy.

He mumbles endearments against my lips. He laps at my hole. He sucks at my clit. He whispers promises against my inner thighs and then laps them away with his tongue.

Eventually, I stop trying to be quiet. I hope Maria and Gabriele are sound sleepers because I can't stop moaning as Alfonso turns onto his back and shimmies between my legs, spreading me wider to accommodate the broad shoulders that clearly run in his family. There's no going back after that.

He pulls my pussy down onto his face, licking and sucking at me for all he's worth.

When I rise onto my knees and sit fully on his face, he groans. The vibrations of his arousal against my sex is divine. Somehow or other, nothing and no one has ever felt as good as this. Alfonso's lips circle my clit, and he sucks as hard as he can.

"Oh fuck, fuck, fuck," I scream.

His right hand sinks into my stomach, his left into my hip. He holds me as I begin to ride his tongue until finally, I'm coming directly into his mouth.

I feel the warm splatter of his come on my back.

"Fuck, you're amazing," I breathe.

"Il sentiment è reciproco," he murmurs against my clit.

Someone bangs on the door and calls out in Italian.

Alfonso sighs, and I shiver because that gust of air against my overstimulated sex has me on the verge of another orgasm.

"My mother wants to know if you want eggs. She said all the Americans in movies eat eggs for breakfast."

I fall off of him, laughing loudly.

Alfonso

Zoe is in such a good mood that she doesn't complain even though we have to walk over four hundred steps to the street. She's tired, and sweaty, and beautiful, but she doesn't complain. Probably because Ugo carries her suitcase.

When we make it to the street, Ugo leads the way to his car. It's covered in leaves and dirt because he never uses it. He's like our father, much more comfortable walking or taking his scooter.

"Don't crash it," he teases as he lifts Zoe's baggage into the boot.

"I won't," I say with a hint of trepidation. I'm actually a very good driver, but life has a way of spiraling out of control. "I promise."

He rolls his eyes and turns to Zoe. "Sorella," he says softly.

Zoe and I wait for more, but that's it.

For Ugo, it is enough.

He hugs and kisses me before walking back to the steps where he'll ascend the stairs back to the home he shares with our parents and resume the rest of his very normal life.

I will miss him.

I drive down to the beach and park Ugo's car in front of the grocers, where he will pick it up later today. I grab all of our bags and walk with Zoe back to the shore. We climb onto the pier to find Nicola's yacht already there. He jumps down and helps me lug her bag onto the boat. And then we both offer our hands to Zoe. She takes mine.

I help her up the steps, where Nicola helps her onto the deck.

Nicola doesn't banter. Not much, at least. Today, he's driven by the same urgency I feel. We back away from the pier and head out onto the water. "We'll be in Naples before noon," I tell Zoe as I cradle her head in my lap until she falls asleep.

I settle her head on the cushion and then climb into the cockpit.

"What did you do with them?" I ask Nicola.

"Do you really want to know?"

I do, actually, but he's right. The less I know, the better.

"You covered your tracks." It's not a question, but it is.

Nicola smiles at me and winks. "I am not that foolish, fratello."

I squint at him. "Yes, actually, you are."

He laughs, and I laugh.

I've missed this.

Zoe

I can see Naples.

We're in a queue for the pier, and from the water, this city looks beautiful. I hadn't realized that before. But a few days ago feels like a century. I feel like a brand-new person, especially when Alfonso wraps himself around my back.

His bare arms bracket mine. I want to go back to this morning when there was nothing between us.

"I can take you to the airport," he whispers against my ear.

I jerk, but he holds me in place.

"You can go home," he says. "That's what you wanted." I jerk again, and his arms tighten around me. "If you want to go home, you can."

"What the fuck?" I hiss, at a loss for words.

Alfonso wraps his arms around my chest, squeezing me hard enough to keep me still, and also, I think, so that I can remember him holding me this way. His nose and mouth brush against my cheek. "I didn't kidnap you," he whispers.

I shift in his arms, enough to see him out of the corner of my eye but not enough to break his hold on me. "What do you want?"

He shakes his head and sighs.

"Tell me."

I feel his struggle. The desire to keep this from me, to *not* follow my order. But he can't. And I can't describe what that does to me.

"I want you to stay," he whispers. His mouth moves to my ear. "I want you to want to stay."

Nicola calls to us. We're docking. I see someone jumping and waving. It takes me a few moments to realize that I'm looking at my sister. I've never seen her this happy.

I've never been this happy.

I rest my nails against the back of Alfonso's hand. "Last night, when you were inside me, I decided to stay in Italy for a little while longer," I say, and he groans. And then I scrape my nails down his hand, and he moans into my ear, his hips pressing forward into my ass. "Glad you're catching up."

Zahra

"So, how was Positano?" I ask, even though I can guess by the way Alfonso is holding onto my sister's hand. He looks like he'll punch a hole in anyone who gets too close to her.

She rolls her eyes. "I'm sorry," she says.

My mouth falls open. "What?"

"I said I'm sorry." She rolls her eyes again before looking at me with sincerity in her gaze. "Sorry I came here to bring you home. That's not my job. From here on out, I just want to be your sister. Not another auntie."

I'm at a loss for words, and there are tears in my eyes.

"Amore," Giulio whispers.

"If you hug me, I'm going to take it all back," Zoe warns.

So I throw myself into Alfonso's shocked arms. "Oh my God, thank you," I tell him. "I don't know what you did. I mean, I can guess. Please keep doing that. Thank you."

Zoe sighs irritably.

Giulio has to pull me off of him. "Stay away from her," he tells Alfonso.

The other man looks ruffled and bewildered.

"Thank you," I say again, emotion making my voice break.

"My God, are you pregnant too?" Zoe shrieks.

"Zahra?" Giulio gasps.

And I roll my eyes at him. "Still on birth control," I sigh. "You know this."

"Hallelujah, amen," Zoe breathes.

Giulio

We head straight to the airport.

Normally, we would never travel together, but these are special circumstances.

"How long?" Alfonso asks, his face red with fury.

I hadn't wanted to tell him this yesterday. I was hoping it wouldn't be true by the time he returned. I wasn't so lucky. "I haven't heard from Salvo in nearly forty hours."

He curses, and he has a reason to. If Andrea was telling the truth and the Serpente Nero has decided to turn on him, we might be too late to save him; he and Shae and their baby might already be dead.

"Oh my God, this is amazing," Zoe says.

We turn to see her and Zahra sharing a box of hot zeppole.

"Right?" Zahra laughs.

Alfonso and I don't talk about what we will tell them. If we're right — if we're too late — nothing we say will heal this wound.

Grand Theft N.Y.E.

The Family

Beautiful and Dirty

The Hitman

The Enforcer

Dolci

Bay Area Blues

Layover

Back in the Day

Standalone stories

Encore

Office Hours

The Tenant

Sex Toy Soldier

Looking [Patreon exclusive]